What terrible secret was destroying Pascale?

It was unthinkable. She had to protect Rémi at all costs. Pascale abandoned herself to the fervor of total sacrifice. She felt as if she were being enveloped and penetrated by a dazzling light.

She opened her eyes. Why did the people gathered closely around her seem to be so incredibly far away? What was that police inspector shouting at her through the dense fog that surrounded him?

"You killed her out of jealousy! Admit it!"

"It's true," she said in a barely audible voice.

Then she fainted and slid from her chair to the floor.

House of Secrets

by DENISE NOEL

NEW YORK • TORONTO

HOUSE OF SECRETS/first published August 1977.

Second printing October 1977
Third printing March 1978

ISBN 0-373-90001-5

PRINTED IN CANADA

Chapter 1

As usual, the six-o'clock train from Paris to suburban Versailles filled quickly. The first wave of commuters piled into the empty seats; the latecomers leaned wearily on the doors and backs of seats or against the people standing next to them. Listless eyes stared vacantly at the drab station outside. Many of the commuters were absorbed with pleasant inner visions of what they would be doing soon after they reached their suburban homes: weeding the lettuce patch, watering the geraniums, reading or simply relaxing after their day in the city.

Some of them opened magazines and newspapers to pass the time. One man took a Versailles weekly from his pocket.

"Did you see this ad? The Sévrier house is for sale."

Passengers on that commuter train often joined in each other's conversations, especially when the topic was something that stirred their curiosity. The name of Sévrier recalled a tragedy to them—a tragedy that had caused a sensation in Versailles the year before.

Some had known the people involved and they all knew the setting: a beautiful mansion on the Avenue de Paris. They had often admired its wrought-iron gate and colorful flower beds. It still looked like a house that could shelter only happiness within its walls.

"What a terrible thing to happen to such a nice man!" exclaimed one woman.

Everyone in Versailles could claim to have seen Rémi Sévrier, the famous lawyer, at least once.

"Charges dismissed!" sneered a resentful voice. "That shows you how lawyers and judges all stick together."

Other voices protested indignantly.

"The charges *had* to be dismissed. There was no case against Pascale Nolay."

"She was innocent! Anyone could see that!"

"A trial would have been a waste of time. Any jury would have acquitted her."

Jerking and squeaking, the train started off.

"I'll tell you one thing," a plump, middle-aged woman confided solemnly, "they all suffered, even though they were rich. If you're born unlucky, all the money in the world can't make you happy."

In the train's only first-class car, conversation had taken on a slightly different tone.

"Have you heard that the Sévrier house is for sale?"

"I saw the ad in the paper."

"That ought to put an end to the whole thing at last. There's been far too much talk about it."

"At least the press was fairly discreet. . . . Come to think of it, you were a neighbor of Rémi Sévrier, so you must have seen Pascale Nolay."

"No, I never did. Not that I remember, anyway."

"I did," interjected a woman dressed with showy elegance. "I recognized her picture in the papers. A pretty young brunette. I saw her in Trianon Park several times. She used to take Etienne there. He was a sweet little boy. My son played with him often."

At the front end of the car with her back to the other passengers, a young woman had been listening to all this. Her slender, graceful figure was adorned with a simple but well-made blue linen dress, and her short brown hair framed a triangular face with delicate features. A mocking glint appeared in her expressive hazel eyes. *People are so silly!* she thought. *Either that woman is imagining things or she's lying just to make an impression. I never took Etienne to play in Trianon Park.*

She sat up straighter. The fear of being recognized that had begun to obsess her as soon as she boarded the train relaxed its grip on her. There was no need to worry. The picture the papers had published at the time of her arrest hardly looked like her at all, and none of the people who had known her in Versailles would be there now: it was July, long past the time when they went to their summer homes.

"Everyone in Versailles was surprised when the charges were dismissed," a woman said harshly. "In my opinion, that girl should have been brought to trial."

Pascale shuddered and slumped down in her seat again. She hadn't realized that complete strangers still harbored such strong memories and opinions about something that had happened more than eight months ago.

But a few days ago, a small advertisement in a Paris newspaper was enough to reawaken that part of her past. Rémi Sévrier's house was going to be sold.

Pascale, who had just returned from a long stay in the mountains, had learned the news from her mother the day before.

Since her return, Pascale's sisters had treated her with warm and unaccustomed affection. To avoid stirring up painful memories, they had made no mention of the tragedy. But despite all their efforts to cheer her up they were unable to drive away the sorrow that darkened her eyes.

Lambert, her long-time friend, came to have lunch with the Nolays as soon as he learned she was back. He still had the same ungainly walk and the same look of carefree happiness on his likable face. His liveliness and sparkling wit usually made Pascale look on the bright side of things. But even his stimulating company could not bring back her good spirits.

"Let's close up the store," her mother had said in a final attempt to dispell Pascale's gloom, "and take a vacation—all six of us. We'll just get in the car and go wherever we feel like going, and stay as long as we like. That should make Pascale forget what happened in Versailles. Afterward she can go back to medical school or, if she'd rather, she can work with us in the store." Since her husband's death Madame Nolay and her three grown-up daughters had run an antique shop near the Luxembourg Gardens in Paris.

Camille, Simone, Gisele and Lambert had all agreed enthusiastically.

There had been a long silence during which Pascale was close to tears. But her voice had been firm when she answered, "All right, I'll do it, but first I want to go back to Versailles one last time."

The wave of family disapproval did not change her mind. She hadn't yet come to any decisions about her future, but for the moment a compelling need drove her back to the house in which she had suffered so much.

Why? she wondered as she leaned her aching head against the back of the train seat. *I should try to forget that place completely. Why am I going there? To pick up a few belongings I don't need?*

She was too honest with herself to accept that flimsy pretext. In her heart she knew why she was returning to the big, deserted house, now kept by only a pair of servants. She had to see the study where Rémi had worked, once again inhale its aroma of leather, wax and English tobacco, touch the objects he had held in his hand. . . .

Images of the tragedy drifted before her eyes. Why had she passively accepted the accusations of the police? Why hadn't she revealed the truth when she was questioned? She could have cleared herself by simply describing what she had seen. Her love for Rémi had kept her silent. She had narrowly escaped being put on trial, and even after the charges against her were dismissed she had still been violently condemned by people who only vaguely understood what had really happened. But that humiliation was nothing compared to the pain that engulfed her.

Suddenly aware that she was twisting her train ticket out of shape, she tried to put together what was left of it. Then, with startling clarity, a similar scene burst into her memory. Once before, during another trip to Versailles, she had absent-mindedly torn up a ticket and had had great trouble assembling the pieces.

Her headache gradually gave way to a dreamy torpor. The rhythmic clacking of the wheels turned into a gentle murmur. The present faded into images from the past: she was on that same train, looking out the window at those same suburban houses, wearing that same blue linen dress, thinking happily of the vacation that lay ahead.

She never could have guessed that she was on her way to a terrifying adventure. . . .

Chapter 2

"Are you Pascale Nolay? I'm Serge, Monsieur Sévrier's chauffeur."

A middle-aged man wearing a navy blue uniform bowed to her as she came out of the small station.

She stopped, surprised. "Yes, I'm Pascale Nolay, but how did you know who to look for in this crowd?"

Serge smiled and took her suitcases.

"The people who usually take this train don't have so much baggage, except when they're coming back from vacation, so it was easy to pick you out of the crowd. If you'll wait for me here, I'll bring the car. I had to park it over there."

Pascale watched him walk toward a black Rolls-Royce. She couldn't help smiling when she remembered the modest Citroën the Sévriers had owned in the past. But she wasn't surprised by their new wealth: several years earlier Rémi Sévrier had inherited his father's great fortune. He and his family had then left their Paris apartment and moved into a house in Versailles. Pascale had learned this from Mutual Aid, an organization that provided babysitting jobs for students.

When she was still in high school, Pascale had often taken care of the Sévriers' year-old son, Etienne. When Monsieur Sévrier's law practice became more successful, and the inheritance had allowed the move to Versailles, the family had hired a full-time nursemaid. They hadn't used the services of Mutual Aid for the past three years.

But chance brought Pascale back to little Etienne.

Two days earlier, Madame Nolay had gathered all four of her daughters together—a difficult task because Camille, Simone and Gisèle were often away attending antique auctions. All three of Pascale's sisters were over thirty. They had plain faces, graceless bodies and hearts without a great deal of tenderness. None of them regretted not being married. They were businesswomen, and independence was more attractive to them than family life.

Pascale, the youngest, was quite different. With her short nose and rather wide mouth, she wasn't classically beautiful, but she had become a radiant young woman. Her slender form, graceful movements and gentle charm attracted attention. Courage and honesty showed in her lovely hazel eyes and everyone who knew her felt the warmth she radiated.

The Nolays weren't rich. The antique shop barely made a decent living for them. Since business didn't appeal to Pascale, she had chosen another occupation. With her sympathetic heart, she wanted to care for sick people or children. Left to her own inclinations, she would have applied for a job in a nursery school, because she had no desire to spend long years studying to become a doctor. But her mother and sisters had more ambitious plans for her. They had kept urging her to go to medical school until she finally gave in. And now, at twenty-four, she was well on her way to becoming a physician.

Finally the whole family was gathered in the apartment—four large but dark rooms at the back of a courtyard on the Boulevard Malesherbes. Madame Nolay told her daughters: "I'm afraid we can't take a vacation this summer. There will be too many antiques sales near Paris that we can't afford to miss, and we'll need all the money we can possibly scrape together. We can take off a week or two at the end of the year, but I think it would be foolish for us to go away now. Are you willing to stay?"

The three oldest daughters were entirely willing. Pascale had been dreaming of escaping the city for a vacation in the country or at the seaside but she gave up her plans without complaint because she realized the limits of the family budget.

The school year was just ending, so it was too late to apply for a job as counselor in a children's camp, as she had done several times in the past. Then she thought of Mutual Aid. When she went there, she was pleasantly surprised to learn that Madame Sévrier wanted a young woman to take care of her son for the summer.

Pascale remembered little Etienne as a delightful child with dark, curly hair. She applied for the job and Monsieur Sévrier called her that evening.

When she had worked as the Sévriers' babysitter five years earlier, she had met the elegant Madame Sévrier and her sister, Irène Deville, who lived with the family and seemed to run the household. She knew Rémi Sévrier only from the pictures that appeared in newspapers when he was involved in an important case in court. She imagined him as a rather inaccessible, intimidating man.

But her apprehension vanished when she heard his deep, friendly voice on the telephone.

"If you still think of Etienne as a gentle little angel," he said, "you'd better revise that image. He's six now, and he's turned into a little demon, the kind of child who'd push Little Red Riding Hood into the wolf's jaws. Are you frightened?"

She laughed.

"No, children never frighten me."

She wasn't told exactly what her duties would be, but she didn't care whether she acted as a nursemaid or a governess. She knew only that she and Etienne would go to the Sévriers' country estate in Les Landes, and that was enough to make her happy.

THE ROLLS-ROYCE passed through the open gateway, rolled along a broad drive bordered by spindle trees, then skirted a freshly mowed lawn that encircled a bed of red begonias.

Pascale looked at the white stone house set into the greenery of the park like a jewel in a luxurious case. Three tall, arched French doors opening onto a balustraded terrace gave it a majestic air. The second-floor windows were adorned with elegant wrought-iron balconies.

The chauffeur stopped the car and walked around to open the door for her. A maid hurried down the terrace steps.

"Please come with me, Mademoiselle."

Pascale cast an admiring glance around her. A privet hedge and a screen of leafy elms muffled the sounds of traffic and isolated the park from the street.

The air was filled with the insistent chirping of birds. The whole setting gave her a feeling of calm and harmony.

Inside the house, that feeling was heightened by an impression of comfortable luxury: a light, beautifully proportioned entrance hall, a broad staircase with delicately wrought banisters, period furniture, soft carpets, numerous works of art.

"Monsieur Sévrier will see you in a moment," said the maid. "Please wait in here."

She opened the double doors and Pascale went into a large study and library. On the opposite side two French doors opened onto the park. She could smell the fragrance of a nearby rose garden. Dark books lined the walls to the ceiling and gilded mahogany Empire furniture gave the room a solemn atmosphere that was unexpectedly lightened by the bust of Cicero on the mantelpiece: a jockey cap was tilted at a rakish angle on top of the august Roman's head. The maid quickly flipped it off as she was leaving the room.

"Etienne has been here again," she said, smiling at Pascale. "I'll take away the evidence. This wouldn't be a good day for him to get another scolding."

Without any further explanations, she slipped the cap into her apron pocket and closed the door quietly behind her.

Pascale was puzzled. Why hadn't she been taken to Madame Sévrier or, if she was out, to her sister, Mademoiselle Deville? Wouldn't either of them be better able to outline her duties than Monsieur Sévrier?

She didn't have much time to wonder about it. A tall figure came in through one of the French doors.

She stood, feeling a little intimidated; but the man's warm smile immediately put her at ease. His regular features were almost too handsome. At first she thought Rémi Sévrier surprisingly youthful, but as he spoke she noticed strands of silver in the dark, slightly wavy hair and saw fine lines that time, or sorrow, had engraved on his forehead and around his mouth. There was a trace of gentle sadness in his eyes. He looked at her with attentive curiosity.

"You've taken on a very difficult task." He sighed as he moved an armchair and sat in front of her. "That's why I wanted to talk to you personally, to warn you about the problems you'll come up against. If you feel they're too much to cope with, you can forget the agreement we made on the phone.

"Taking care of Etienne is no simple matter. For the past year or so he's been doing everything imaginable to make himself unbearable. He's unruly, hot-tempered and insolent. Punishment rolls off him like water off a duck's back. He simply ignores it and does the same thing again as soon as he gets the chance."

"Is he a bit spoiled, perhaps?" suggested Pascale. "Some children need to be raised with great firmness."

Amusement glimmered in Rémi Sévrier's eyes.

"How old are you?" he asked.

"Twenty-four."

He leaned toward her.

"It's easy to concoct theories about child rearing when you've had no experience. Wait till you've had to deal with a little hellion like my son; then you'll see what happens to your theories. Neither strictness nor tenderness has any effect on him. He rebels against every attempt to reach him. He's had a long series of experienced, well-qualified governesses and they all made efforts to correct his faults. The most tenacious lasted only six weeks."

He paused and fixed her with penetrating look.

"In view of all that," he went on, smiling kindly, "you must be wondering why I contacted a student-employment agency this time, rather than one that specializes in highly trained governesses."

"Is it because you don't want another governess with rigid principles? You want someone who'll just love your son and try to understand him."

She spoke fervently, convinced that she could succeed where others had failed.

He took her hands in his.

"You're very perceptive," he said gently. "It reassures me to know you guessed almost exactly what I had in mind. I say 'almost' because I'm not asking you to stay here as a governess. Clotilde, the maid who met you at the door, will go on taking care of Etienne as far as the practical work is concerned. Since it's vacation time, you won't be giving him any lessons. That's probably just as well—three governesses have given up on him this year. It's not that he's incapable of learning, but he works only when he feels like it and most of the time he's so stubborn he'd try the patience of a saint, as my sister-in-law says.

"I'd like you to be something like an older sister to him. I've told him a friend was coming to live with us for a while. Soon you and Etienne will go to Estello, our estate in Les Landes where he usually spends his vacations; my wife's sister will be with you to handle all the details of running the estate. She's a very capable woman but I can't expect her to take on the extra burden of looking after a child as difficult as Etienne. My wife and I will be in Switzerland most of the summer because of some important business I have there."

"I'll do my best for Etienne," Pascale assured him

earnestly, "and I'm sure it won't be too difficult for me."

"I certainly hope you're right!"

After examining her attentively for a few moments, he sensed the honesty and integrity that shone from her eyes. A delicate face, radiant with charm, confirmed his growing confidence in her.

He seemed about to say something, then changed his mind. Instead,he stood, clasped his hands behind his back and began pacing the floor in worried silence.

Pascale didn't know what to think. She remembered the maid putting Etienne's cap in her pocket so he wouldn't be scolded. For a moment she wondered if the servants might not have more affection for the child than his parents did. Perhaps his father's reluctance to talk about him was simply lack of concern. She soon realized her mistake when he stopped his pacing and stood in front of her with an expression of deep distress.

"I have to tell you more about Etienne. I love him dearly, but sometimes he frightens me. The things he does don't always seem like childish pranks. This morning, for example, when Clotilde wasn't watching, he let his mother's Pekinese out into the street, knowing full well that cars always threw it into a panic. The inevitable happened: the dog was run over and killed. It was a terrible shock to my wife. She was so upset she had to go to her room to lie down, and she's still there. But Etienne hasn't shown the slightest trace of emotion. No tears, no regret. Don't you think it's alarming to see such cold-blooded cruelty in a six-year-old child?"

"Let's hope appearances don't tell the real story," soothed Pascale. "Maybe he really didn't do it out of cruelty." She thought frantically for a few moments.

"He may have turned the dog loose accidentally, then felt so guilty about what happened because of his carelessness that he hid his unhappiness by acting as if he didn't care. Was he given a severe scolding?"

Rémi ignored the question. He sat on a corner of his desk and asked, "What would you have done in my place?"

Pascale was disconcerted.

"Well," she said hesitantly, "I might have tried to reason with him, or I might have punished him, or . . . I don't know. I guess I would have just let the circumstances guide me and hope I acted wisely."

"What if circumstances show you that nothing you do has any effect on Etienne?"

She waved that possibility aside.

"Until I see for myself, I won't believe any child is incorrigible."

"Since my warnings haven't shaken your optimism," said Rémi, "I'll give up trying to discourage you . . . I don't really want to, you know. Would you like a cigarette?"

He picked up a black lacquered box, opened it and held it out to her.

"No, thank you."

He took a cigarette from the box and closed it. She stared at the gold plumes that decorated its lid. A long-lost memory nudged her mind.

As he lit his cigarette, Rémi saw her looking intently at the box. He gestured toward it.

"It's from the seventeenth century, a real collector's item. It's beautiful, isn't it?"

A strange smile passed over Pascale's face.

"Isn't it by the Japanese master, Korin?"

"Yes, it is," he said, surprised. "You must be a real expert on—"

She interrupted him with a laugh.

"No, I don't know anything about Japanese antiques. But when I was a child my mother had a box like that for sale in her store. It fascinated me. I was always imagining all sorts of wondrous things, and somehow I got it into my head that the black box contained a genie like the one in Aladdin's lamp. I can still remember how horrified my sisters were whenever they caught me playing with it. They always told me it was a real Korin and I wasn't allowed to touch it."

"And when your mother sold it," finished Rémi, "you showed your disapproval by promising dire calamities to the poor buyer, as if it were Pandora's box."

"How did you know that?" she asked in amazement.

A playful smile made his face look younger.

"Nearly twenty years ago my father discovered that box in an antique store near the Luxembourg Gardens. I was with him the day he went there to buy it. I remember the little girl who had a temper tantrum and shrieked insults at me."

Pascale listened in stunned silence, recalling the image of a middle-aged man accompanied by his adolescent son who clutched the precious box against his chest. She was embarrassed, but at the same time all distance between them seemed abolished by that memory they shared.

"I think I even kicked you," she said shamefacedly.

"You probably did! You were beside yourself with rage. My father was amused by the richness of your vocabulary. You told me a demon would take vengeance on me if I took the box away."

"I must have seemed like a nasty little brat to you! I'm glad you didn't let yourself be influenced by my threats."

"Who knows?" he murmured, as though to himself. "I might have been better off if I had listened to you. They say that truth comes from the mouths of babes. . . ."

His half-closed eyes seemed to be watching some painful, inner vision. She saw his face become tense. A moment later he relaxed and smiled at her again.

"Since it turns out we've 'known' each other for twenty years," he smiled, "the story I told Etienne is almost true. A friend has come to stay here a while. I'm glad we've made such a good start . . . but I'm sure you'd like to unpack your things now. Clotilde will show you to your room."

He stood and pushed a button beside the fireplace. His gray suit and white shirt gave him a distinguished, almost austere elegance, but any impression of severity was offset by his friendly smile and the casual ease of his movements.

As she watched him walk lithely across the room and bend down to pick up a sheet of paper that had fallen off his desk, he seemed more like a tennis player than an eminent lawyer. A very likable man, she decided, surprised to realize that she felt as if they already knew each other very well.

"Will it be all right for me to go and say hello to Madame Sévrier?" she asked.

"Yes, of course, but she'll see you in her room. She's so upset about the dog that she won't come downstairs this evening. Her sister is staying with her. I have to leave soon, so you may prefer to have dinner in your room. I'm afraid the dining room will seem a little depressing if you eat there alone."

"But what about Etienne?"

"He doesn't come to our table yet. He eats in the kitchen."

There was a knock at the door.

"Come in." A maid appeared. "Ah, it's you, Berthe. Is Clotilde busy?"

"She's giving Etienne his dinner."

"Very well. Please take Mademoiselle Nolay upstairs to Madame."

Berthe looked at him in surprise.

"Madame left about fifteen minutes ago."

"In her car?"

"Yes, sir. She's spending the evening with some friends who are going to find another dog for her. Didn't you know?"

He snapped his fingers with sudden annoyance.

"Yes, of course. It slipped my mind. . . . Tell Serge I'm almost ready to leave." He glanced at his watch and turned to Pascale. "I have to go to Paris now, for a business dinner. Excuse me for leaving you so quickly."

There was a note of impatience in his voice. A tense, withdrawn, irritable man had replaced the friend who had talked with Pascale a few moments earlier. He bowed stiffly and left the room without looking back.

Trying to drive away the strange uneasiness that had just come over her, Pascale asked the maid to take her to Etienne.

Chapter 3

Pascale sat at her desk, lost in thought for a moment. Lambert was such a dear friend. Perhaps a letter describing her new life would help her unravel the many impressions she had received. She smiled briefly, almost hearing Lambert's indignant response to the Sévrier family, and picked up her pen.

Dear Lamb,

Maybe I'm becoming foolishly sentimental—I left my friends only six days ago, and I miss them already. Not that I have any reason to complain about the Sévriers. They're very friendly to me and treat me exactly as if I were a member of the family. For example, when Monsieur Sévrier talks to me about his wife or his sister-in-law he refers to them as Andrea and Irène. And they in turn call him Rémi when discussing him with me.

So you were wrong when you said I'd be treated

like an inferior. I don't feel at all lonely here. I want to give you my impressions because I think they're strange enough to interest you, and I'd like to know what you make of them. Watching the Sévriers is like seeing one of those odd, disjointed films that don't make sense till the very end. So far I haven't been able to figure out why they act the way they do.

Since you're an abstract sculptor and you've often explained to me how you try to make the soul appear in the unusual forms you create, I'd like to see you practise your art here; they all act, talk and smile as if playing parts. Their conversations are friendly but hollow. They never seem to say what they're really thinking. They all wear masks.

Andrea Sévrier would fascinate you. She has blond hair and a lovely, angelic face with a delicate nose, a velvety complexion and perfectly shaped lips. She's a beautiful, gracious, refined and elegant woman, but when she smiles there's a vacant look in her violet eyes that makes me feel uneasy. I can't tell if she's lost in some secret dream or if her mind is simply empty. She reminds me of a mechanical doll that used to be in my mother's store: she has the same exquisite features and the same lack of expression.

But yesterday I saw her mask crack. We were having coffee in the drawing room after lunch when Rémi announced that he had found a buyer for the country house he owns near Deauville. He seemed glad to be able to sell it, but Andrea acted as if he had slapped her in the face. She stood up in a livid rage and banged her cup down on the table so hard it broke.

"Try not to be so clumsy, Andrea," Irène warned her gently.

They looked at each other for a few seconds; then they smiled with a kind of secret understanding. It was the first time I'd ever seen any warmth in Andrea's face.

Rémi didn't seem to attach any importance to the incident. He stood up calmly enough and went to ring for one of the maids.

He's still a mystery to me. He was very friendly when I first came here. He told me how worried he was about his son's unruly behavior and I had the impression he'd be watching closely to see if there was any improvement. But since then he seems to have lost interest in Etienne and hasn't asked me a single question about him. He's away most of the time, and when he's here he seems so preoccupied and depressed. Sometimes he just stares at Andrea without saying anything. I think he's deeply in love with her, perhaps unfortunately so, because she leads a very free life.

Irène Deville, Andrea's sister, is another puzzling character. She must be a good twenty years older than Andrea. She's short, ugly and sickly. Her eyes are so close together that she almost looks cross-eyed. She has thin, washed-out blond hair that she wears in a bun. She apparently has a strong sweet tooth, because she munches candy from morning till night. There's always something shifty about her expression. She clasps her hands when she talks and she has the unpleasant habit of bowing her head at the end of a sentence, so that you can hardly hear what she's saying. I instinctively avoid her as much as I can.

Since Andrea's social life keeps her away from home so much, Irène runs the household and gives orders in a rather soft, whining voice. The staff is quite large. Besides the two maids, there is also a cook, a chauffeur, and a gardener, who lives here with his wife. The servants don't like Irène but they respect her. Etienne is the only one who rebels against her. She detests him and the feeling is mutual.

What a little demon he is! His father warned me about him but I still wasn't prepared for what I found. On the day I came, he'd let his mother's dog escape, either deliberately or accidentally. The dog was killed by a car.

When I first saw him, he was sitting down to dinner in the kitchen. In his pajamas, all pink from his bath, he looked adorable. Although you've never been interested in children, I don't think you could have resisted this one, with his dark, curly hair, his big eyes and his plump, vigorous little body. He would have tempted you to try your talent as a sculptor, and for all I know he might even have turned you away from abstract art.

Clotilde, one of the maids, told Etienne to stand up to say hello to me. For a second I saw a glow of curiosity in his eyes; then his face went blank and he sat perfectly still, as if he hadn't heard.

Clotilde reached out to take him by the arm but I stopped her and asked her to leave me alone with him. When she was gone, I sat down at the table across from him.

"What a good dinner!" I said. "Soup, a soft-boiled egg, green beans and yogurt. Just looking at it makes me feel hungry as a wolf!"

I held out his bib to him. Instead of taking it, he put both hands behind his back and looked at me defiantly.

"Don't you know how to put it on yourself?" I asked.

His only answer was to wrinkle his nose and

growl. I stood up. He growled louder, with his teeth clenched. Clotilde hurried back into the room and angrily told him to stop acting foolish and eat his dinner.

"I don't know what comes over him sometimes," she explained to me. "Tonight he's probably decided to be a dog. He keeps growling and if you touch him, he bites. I had a terrible time giving him his bath. He shook himself like a dog and splashed water all over the bathroom. He barks instead of talking. He's been acting like that ever since Mademoiselle Irène spanked him. Maybe I should tell Monsieur."

"I don't think so. It would make him too sad to see his little boy changed into a vicious dog." I winked at her. "We'll just have to make the best of it. Let me handle him. I usually get along very well with dogs. You can take away that fork and spoon; he won't need them. A dog laps up his food and it's all mixed together in one dish. Here, I'll show you."

I broke open the soft-boiled egg and mixed it into the soup, along with the yogurt and green beans. Clotilde looked horrified. Etienne watched me in wide-eyed amazement. When I pushed the dish in front of him, his lips quivered as if he was about to burst into tears, but as soon as he saw my mocking expression he gave me another defiant look, put his head down and began noisily lapping up his dinner.

I held up my hand to silence Clotilde, as she was about to say something. You can imagine how nervous I was. I knew the experiment was risky but I was determined to go through with it and accept the consequences.

"Well, I'll leave you now," Clotilde said in a tone

that clearly meant, "Since you got yourself into this mess, you can get yourself out of it."

Etienne looked up at us with food smeared all over his face. Clotilde couldn't help being concerned about him. As she was leaving the room she said, "He can't stand being dirty, and now look at the state he's in! I'll bring a washcloth".

Etienne put his face down over his dish again and blew with all his might, splattering soup all around him. Luckily I stepped back in time to avoid the mess.

Clotilde came back with a wet washcloth and a towel. I stopped her.

"Clotilde, what does a dog do when he's finished eating?"

She decided to humor me.

"Well, let's see. . . . He licks himself and then he goes to sleep."

"That's right, so there's no need to wash him. He'll lick himself clean, like a good dog, and go to his kennel."

Etienne glared at me.

"I'm not a *good* dog!"

"All the more reason for not touching you. I don't want to be bitten."

He answered with a loud growl and jumped up, knocking over his chair. Then, before I realized what was happening he ran out of the pantry on all fours, crossed the kitchen and disappeared into the hall. A few seconds later I heard a scream and then some angry exclamations.

"What happened?" I asked anxiously.

"He must have run into Mademoiselle Irène," answered Clotilde. "There's no telling what kind of trouble he'll make before he goes to bed. I'll be surprised if you get the upper hand."

I offered to put Etienne to bed that night, and she was glad to have me relieve her of the job. She told me how the rooms on the upper floor are arranged.

To the right of the second-floor landing is a hall that leads to three bedrooms, each with its own bathroom. They belong to Rémi, Andrea and Irène. To the left, another hall leads to my room and Etienne's, which have a bathroom between them. Then, around a corner, the hall leads to the linen room and a guest room. On the third floor, some of the rooms are for servants and others are for guests.

As I was about to go upstairs, Irène came bursting into the pantry. She seemed violently angry. Her face was flushed and her eyes were narrowed to two slits. When she recognized me, she forced her thin lips to smile.

"Hello, Pascale," she said. "I hope you'll enjoy your stay with us. If my nephew is sometimes too much for you to handle, let me know and I'll act accordingly."

She turned to Clotilde and held out her left hand. There were two purple marks on her wrist.

"That child is a monster," she hissed with restrained rage. "Look what he just did to me. I found him crawling on the floor in the hall. When I tried to make him stand up, he bit me like a wild animal!"

There was so much hatred and contempt in her voice that I couldn't help coming to Etienne's defense.

"I don't think he's completely responsible for what he did. The accident this afternoon upset him a great deal. Maybe he's decided to become a dog out of an unconscious need to punish himself by taking the place of the victim."

"You sound like a psychoanalyst," she retorted. "You think he bit me to punish himself? With a theory like that, he can be excused for anything."

"I'll try to make him behave better," I soothed, "but I do think his act tonight is a result of the shock he had earlier."

Her hostile expression showed her opinion of my reasoning better than any words could have done. I left without saying anything more and went off to find Etienne.

I peered around the doorway of his room and saw that his bed was empty. I tiptoed inside. He was lying on the floor in a corner with his head on his arms, and his cheeks were wet with tears.

I picked him up as gently as I could but he woke up and looked at me with the most profound despair in his eyes. I put him down on his bed and wiped his face with my handkerchief. He had one last surge of rebelliousness.

"Go away."

"Why?"

"I bite."

"A dog only bites people he's afraid of. You're not afraid of me, are you?"

He frowned and seemed to be lost in thought. I tucked him in and closed the shutters. His voice stopped me as I was leaving the room.

"You mean Youli was afraid of me?"

I came back slowly and leaned over him. He had closed his eyes to hold back two big tears that were welling up under his eyelids. I wondered what terrible image he was struggling against. It was easy to guess who Youli was, but I felt powerless to relieve Etienne of a sorrow that was too big for him to handle.

"Go to sleep now," I said quietly, stroking his forehead.

He opened his eyes and gave me such a helpless, pleading look that I felt like trying to reassure him by telling him I didn't believe he was guilty and I was sure it had only been an accident. But I was afraid it might be a mistake to say anything more, so I only kissed him on the forehead.

He took hold of my hand and squeezed it hard. Suddenly his face took on an expression of anger and stubborn pride. As if he wanted to justify himself and throw off a burden of unbearable remorse, he said fiercely, "Youli was a nasty little dog and I'm glad the car ran over him!" Then he turned over on his side and buried his face in the pillow.

How can I explain such a hostile attitude? Was he just "born bad," as Irène seems to think? I don't believe that at all. I think the trouble is that he's unhappy, and I want to find out why. I'm already fascinated by the problem; and my stay here certainly won't be boring.

Write to me, Lamb. It's odd—when I'm with you I'm sometimes quiet for hours at a time, but when I'm away from you I have a strong need to tell you everything that's on my mind. Is that a sign of childishness, or does it just show that I miss my best friend?

Did you sell some of your works at the Festival of Contemporary Sculpture? Keep me posted on your success.

Love,
Pascale

A few days later, Pascale received a reply from Lambert. She smiled in anticipation as she settled down to read his letter.

Dear Pascale,

I feel terribly jealous of those Sévriers. Why do you let them have the benefit of your intelligence, sensitivity, tenderness and all the other things about you that make me adore you, when you refuse to give them to the only person capable of really appreciating them?

As soon as I realized I wouldn't see you again till the end of summer, the hours became twice as long as before. My life is empty. Without you, I've lost the mysterious leaven that transformed my sculpture into something valid. The forms I create now have no souls.

Abandon that family. Leave Etienne the Terror to his tantrums and go camping with me in Brittany or Savoy. If your foolish prejudices still won't let you lead a free, normal life with a man, consider me not as just a friend, but as your fiancé.

I'm sure you think that's a strange way to propose, but I'm completely sincere. You may object because we don't always have the same tastes and ideas. That's all to the good. Each of us will keep his own personality. They say that's the secret of lasting happiness.

I'll be waiting for your answer.

All my love,

Lamb

P.S. During the festival I nearly sold my most important work, my "Sitting Woman," to a millionaire who made his money in beer. But I finally refused the huge price he offered me because it turned out that the idiot wanted to use my brilliant sculpture as an unusual perch for his parakeets. I told him to go back to his beer and leave art alone.

Second P.S. The fact that you feel like telling me everything that's on your mind isn't a sign of childishness. It shows you love me.

PASCALE SLOWLY FOLDED Lambert's letter and put it down on the little mahogany writing desk in one corner of her room. In the park outside, the sunlight moved the birds to sing. She stepped onto the balcony and let her eyes wander beyond the fragrant bed of roses beneath her window. The letter hadn't aroused much emotion in her. She knew Lambert too well to take him seriously when such an outburst of feeling made him propose to her.

Even so, she was puzzled by his proposal. He was always attacking conventional ideas and claimed to have nothing but contempt for people who "let themselves be roped into marriage."

He must really be bored to tears, she thought, *if he could accept the idea of giving up his freedom even during the time it took him to write that letter.*

It didn't occur to her that his passion might be strong enough to make him willing to change his ways. In the depths of her heart she considered love not as an unthinking impulse but as a deep, powerful feeling based on reason and a solid foundation, even though it first came from an irresistible attraction. In her opinion, no such feeling could develop between her and Lambert because they disagreed on too many things.

He was five years older than Pascale. He was born in the Burgundy village where her grandparents lived. As far back as she could remember, they had been together during her summer vacations there. Her family had offered him hospitality when he came to Paris to study art, and later, when he had moved into a studio on the Left Bank, he had continued to visit them. He and Pascale had a strong friendship that survived arguments and even bitter quarrels. She regarded him with a mixture of harshness and admiration. He was conceited, selfish and fickle, but so overflowing with talent that it was easy to forgive his faults.

But this time, through the friendly words of his letter, his faults appeared so clearly she could see nothing else.

He has no intention of changing anything about his life even after he's married, she thought with a touch of bitterness. *That's what he means when he says, "Each of us will keep his own personality." He's already been swept off his feet by so many women that I can't imagine him being devoted to me forever. . . . No, Lamb, marriage isn't just a summer adventure. I'll tell you what it is.*

She sat down at the desk, staring at the wall for some minutes. Then she bent over her desk and wrote a long letter. After re-reading her admonitions she tore it up.

What's the use? she thought. *He wouldn't understand.*

She wrote a short note saying only that she would think over what he had said and discuss it with him when they saw each other again at the end of summer.

As she was addressing the envelope she was startled by a shrill cry from the park. Suddenly remembering that she had left Etienne near the fountain, she rushed out of her room, leaving the papers scattered over her desk.

A moment later, Irène Deville came out of the linen room and stood still. She waited till Pascale had gone downstairs and out the front door, before moving quietly along the hall.

Then, with the lithe quickness of a cat, she slipped into Pascale's room.

Chapter 4

Etienne hadn't fallen into the basin of the fountain as Pascale feared. He had been thrown in by his father.

When she arrived on the scene, Etienne was splashing around in a foot and a half of water, his clothes dripping. The slippery bottom made it hard for him to get to his feet. Standing at the edge of the basin, with his hands in his pockets, Rémi was watching him, apparently relaxed. But when Pascale came closer she saw that he was breathing heavily and that his nostrils were pinched, as if he had just run a long distance.

He turned toward her.

"Don't be alarmed. He deserved that."

"What did he do?"

"I caught him throwing the gardener's cat into the water. It wasn't the first time, and I warned him that I'd punish him if he ever did it again. Cruelty to an animal is inexcusable. I can't help wondering if Irène isn't right when she says there's no hope for him unless he's enrolled in boarding school for problem children."

Rémi seemed close to tears, but he spoke without anger, in the monotone of someone who was completely disheartened. Pascale hadn't seen him for several days and she was struck by the change in his face: his cheeks were hollow and there were deep lines around his mouth.

She tried to reassure him about Etienne, but she didn't even convince herself. After two weeks of treating the child with affectionate firmness, she hadn't seen any change in Etienne at all: he was still as unruly and hostile as ever. Pascale was beginning to doubt she could accomplish anything.

"Maybe he's too isolated," she suggested. "It's not good for a child to be without friends his own age. I'm not thinking of boarding school. I'm sure that would have a bad effect on a boy as high-strung as Etienne. . . ."

"Why should it have a bad effect?" asked a cool voice behind her. "I agree with Irène. Sending him to boarding school is the only way to control him."

Pascale turned and saw Andrea standing a couple of yards away. She wore a white shantung dress, and her usually pale face was darkened with makeup. Pascale paid silent tribute to her beauty. *Nothing can make her ugly,* she thought, *not even her eye shadow and bright lipstick and heavy makeup. They only add a touch of mystery to her elegance. She's as perfect as a work of art.*

Without even glancing at Etienne as he desperately floundered to get out of the basin, Andrea went on: "I admire you for still having illusions after living with Etienne for two weeks. I lost mine long ago. You think he's too isolated? He has a big park to play in and all the toys a child could want. What more does he need?"

"He needs playmates his own age," Pascale said firmly. "Irène won't let me take him to public parks and no one comes to visit him here. It would do him good to be with other children: playing with them, arguing, even fighting."

Andrea dismissed the idea with an impatient gesture.

"Fighting? He's already had enough of that. Last year he went to a private school to learn to read. Within a week he was expelled for constantly picking fights with other pupils. What's he done this time, to deserve that forced bath?"

Rémi, who had so far ignored his wife's presence, slowly turned and looked at her.

"Isn't it a little late to be worried about him?" he asked sarcastically. "You must have heard him shrieking."

"Why should I have come running?" she retorted aggressively. "I knew Pascale was here. I assumed she'd find out what the trouble was, and I was right."

"What if Etienne had drowned?" He was being unreasonable, even unwise, by arguing in front of the child, but at that moment Rémi seemed unaware of anything other than the confrontation with his wife.

"Nothing ever happens to little monsters like that," spat Andrea. "And stop trying to make me feel guilty!" she added with sudden violence. "*You're* the one who threw him in the water!"

Pascale was chilled less by the tension between Andrea and Rémi than by the apparent callousness they displayed toward their son. She was beginning to see them both in a new light. Andrea pressed her lips tightly together, making her face look harder and giving herself a remote resemblance to her sister. The hollows in Rémi's cheeks had deepened. Looking at him from the side, Pascale saw a vein throbbing in his temple.

"I asked you to stay here but you seem to be dressed to go somewhere," he said to his wife. "It's nearly seven o'clock and we're having dinner at Baron d'Entreval's house this evening. Have you forgotten that?"

"I have a fitting at my dressmaker's in twenty minutes."

"A fitting at such an odd time?"

"Why not?"

"You'll have to cancel it."

"No!"

They looked at each other defiantly in a silence charged with electricity. Pascale saw Rémi take a deep breath and close his eyes as if trying to calm himself. Andrea took a little mirror from her purse and examined her makeup attentively.

"Please don't spoil my evening," Rémi said softly. "Arrange things so that we can get to the baron's house on time."

Andrea gave him an ambiguous look, then turned and walked rapidly to the house.

Rémi stood still for a long time, staring at the rhododendron hedge behind which she had disappeared.

Pascale's scream jolted him out of his torpor.

"Etienne! My God!"

He turned his head and his shout echoed hers.

"Etienne!"

She had already jumped into the basin. A rough spot on the cement bottom made her stumble. She twisted her ankle but ignored the pain. Her throat was tight with anxiety as she waded to where Etienne lay face down in the water.

She was overwhelmed with remorse at her carelessness. Then a wave of anger against Rémi and Andrea swept away all other emotions. It was their monstrous egotism that was to blame. They had been so preoccupied with themselves that they forgot Etienne's existence. *They don't care about him. Rémi is obsessed with his jealousy and Andrea doesn't think about anything but admiring herself.* A sob caught in her throat.

She bent down and picked up the unconscious child. As she turned she bumped into Rémi, who had come after her. He took Etienne from her arms.

"Etienne, my little boy!"

His voice was so grief-stricken that Pascale was instantly ashamed of the judgement she had just passed on him. He *did* love his son! That was obvious from his expression.

"It's my fault," she cried. "I should have—"

"No, Pascale. I'm the one to blame." His voice betrayed bitterness.

They quickly waded to the edge of the basin and climbed out.

"Run ahead and call Dr. Bernier," he said urgently.

She laid a reassuring hand on his arm.

"I'll take care of Etienne. We mustn't waste any time. He wasn't under water any more than one minute. I'll give him artificial respiration immediately. Lay him down . . . here, on the grass. No, put him on his back."

"I don't understand," Rémi murmured when he had carefully put down his son. "How could it have happened in such shallow water?"

That was exactly what Pascale was wondering. She knelt beside Etienne's inert little body and tilted his head back for resuscitation.

As she forced air into his lungs she remembered him standing near the edge of the basin, angrily pushing wet hair back from his forehead, then suddenly becoming motionless and staring at his parents with a heartrending expression. "Nothing ever happens to little monsters like that." It was when Andrea said those words that Pascale had turned all her attention to the couple.

Etienne had been only two steps away from the edge of the basin. Why had he been in its deepest part only a minute later? Did he want to simulate an accident to frighten his parents, to punish them for ignoring him? *No,* she thought, *he would have given in to the instinct of self-preservation within ten seconds. Unless. . . .* She rejected the terrible suspicion that crossed her mind but felt a little pang in her heart, followed by another surge of anger against the Sévriers for their lack of self-control. *Who knows? Maybe he was wounded so deeply by what he heard that. . . .*

"How could it have happened?" repeated Rémi, when Pascale paused for a moment to catch her breath. "I've never known him to faint or even have a dizzy spell, but fainting is the only possible explanation, isn't it?"

Their eyes met and Pascale knew his thoughts had followed the same course as hers. But without knowing why, she didn't say the comforting words he was hoping to hear. She shrugged her shoulders slightly in a gesture of uncertainty and looked away.

Clotilde's voice provided a diversion.

"My God! I knew an accident had happened when I heard Pascale scream. He's not . . . dead, is he?"

After unsuccessfully trying to calm her, Pascale sent her to bring a blanket.

Etienne was beginning to revive. Finally he moved convulsively and gasped.

Clotilde returned with a soft woolen blanket. Behind her Irène walked, her eyes lowered. The redness of her cheeks was the only sign of her agitation. She stopped in front of Rémi, clasped her hands and looked on in disapproving silence as he wiped Etienne's face.

"Go put more covers on Etienne's bed," Pascale said to Clotilde, "then tell the cook to make some hot tea."

Irène laughed mockingly and shrugged her narrow shoulders.

"A spanking would do him more good," she said with restrained anger. "It would stimulate his circulation and it might even give him a little respect for authority."

Pascale looked at her in shocked surprise. Irène immediately put her hand over her mouth.

Etienne sneezed. Pascale began rubbing him vigorously through the blanket she had wrapped around him.

"Well, he's managed to gather an audience around him again," said Irène. "You seem really upset, Rémi! That's ridiculous. He got what he deserved. Maybe it will teach him a lesson, but I doubt it."

Rémi stood up.

"Shut up, Irène," he said curtly. "Where's Andrea?"

She looked down to hide the animosity that flared in her eyes. A network of fine lines radiated from her compressed lips. She crossed her hands over her chest.

"She went to her dressmaker's," she answered grudgingly.

"Do you know the phone number?"

"Of course."

"Give it to me. I want her to know that Etienne almost died while we were arguing."

Pascale again felt anger against Rémi. He seemed to be in the grip of an obsession and wouldn't hesitate to sacrifice anything to it. He was intelligent, handsome and apparently in complete control of himself, yet he let himself be dominated by this degrading jealousy.

He looked at Irène with eyes that had turned to steel.

The shadow of a smile played over Irène's lips.

"Let's not be overdramatic," she said. "I don't know why you threw Etienne into the basin, but I'm sure you were right to do it. It's not your fault that it turned out badly, and it's not Andrea's or Pascale's either. I'll show you one reason why he deserved to be punished. Look at this." She raised her upper lip, revealing a tooth with one corner broken off. "Who replaced most of the candy in the crystal vase with pebbles? And who ate that candy? Two pounds of it! No wonder he got sick and fainted! Since you consider it so important for Andrea to know about it, I'll call her, but I don't mind telling you that I think it's silly to disturb her."

She turned away and walked back toward the house with quick little steps.

"Indigestion!" Rémi said to Pascale. "Could that be why he fainted? Sometimes the truth is so much simpler than anything that occurs to you. . . . Thanks to your presence of mind, we avoided the worst. I'll never forget that, Pascale."

His face was hollow with anxiety but he forced a false brightness into his voice. But Pascale knew that even if Etienne had fainted, he had deliberately moved away from the edge of the basin. She smiled thinly back at Rémi.

Chapter 5

At nine o'clock the next morning, Pascale was called to Rémi's study.

Outside, the hot sun was shining on the front of the house. All the venetian blinds on that side were closed. In the study, facing west, orange light filtered through the lowered awnings. Although all the windows were open, no breath of air relieved the heat in the room.

When Pascale came in, she saw Rémi standing beside the mantelpiece, wearing a riding habit.

"Would you like to go out and sit in the shade while we talk?" he asked.

"It's even hotter outside," she said. "A little while ago I went out to pick some flowers for the drawing room and I felt as if I were in an oven."

"What's Etienne up to this morning?"

"Clotilde is giving him a cool bath."

She sat on the leather-covered sofa in one corner of

the room, between two French doors. She was wearing a skirt and a rather heavy tunic. She would have preferred something cooler but the night before someone had maliciously cut up the only two summer blouses she had brought with her. She remembered, too late, what Irène had told her: "Never leave scissors or string where Etienne can find them. With scissors he'll ruin your clothes, and with string he'll set traps that may make you break a leg."

She had unsuspectingly lent him a pair of scissors when he told her he wanted to cut some pictures out of a magazine. When she discovered what he had done with them, she was less upset by the loss of her blouses than by a bitter feeling of failure. Like the governesses who had preceded her, she had been unable to win Etienne's affection.

But she sensed that his malice was only a means of hiding some mysterious anguish. An irresistible inner force drove him to make others miserable but she was sure he felt strong remorse afterward and that only his pride kept him from showing it. Several times she had seen a glimmer of distress in his eyes as he looked at her defiantly. And often, at night, when she came to make sure he was asleep, she found his pillow wet with tears.

Until the accident the day before, she had attributed his strange behavior to his upbringing. She felt he didn't share enough in family life. He had spent most of his time with governesses and maids, cut off from parents who were too absorbed in their own concerns to give him the affection he longed for. But after the accident in the basin she was forced to change her mind. Etienne didn't seem tormented only by a need for affection. The problem wasn't as simple as she had thought. Andrea had hurried home as soon as she learned what had happened, but when she came to his bedside and kissed him, he showed no reaction and lay there with his eyes closed and his face stubbornly turned away from her.

Although she hadn't yet given in to discouragement, Pascale was beginning to feel less certain that she could transform the little wolf into a lamb.

Rémi sat down facing her.

"You should have come riding with me early this morning. The woods were delightfully cool. Do you like to ride?"

"Yes, very much."

"I'm sure you're an excellent rider. You give such an impression of balance and health that you must be good at all sports."

She smiled but didn't protest. Her cheeks flushed as much from embarrassment as from the heat. Her only concession to coquettishness was a touch of powder on the freckles that her first exposure to the summer sun had brought out. She had had her brown hair cut short. Energetically brushed, it fluffed out naturally around her face.

Rémi looked at her warmly and asked, "Would you like to go riding every morning before breakfast?"

Her eyes shone with pleasure. She had always enjoyed riding and regretted that she couldn't do it more often. She imagined herself riding along a bridle path with dew still glistening on the ground, listening to the birds singing in the cool morning air. She gladly accepted Rémi's offer.

"But I thought we were going to leave for Estello the day after tomorrow," she said a moment later.

"Irène wants to have her tooth fixed, so your trip will have to be postponed two or three weeks. You'll probably leave at about the same time I do. Etienne will be sorry for what he's done, because he loves to be at Estello. It will be a more effective punishment than any sermon I could give him."

He paused to light a cigarette, then went on with a worried frown: "I've been thinking over what you said about him yesterday. It's true that he ought to have playmates, although I don't think his isolation has affected his behavior very much. But he's six years old now. We can't go on keeping him away from children his age. We must—"

He stopped short and looked out toward the park. A moment later Andrea appeared in one of the open doorways, wearing sandals, tight yellow pants and a matching blouse, with a tiny dog in her arms.

"I can't stand this heat any longer," she protested. "I'm going to Deauville tomorrow. Just because the house has been sold. . . ."

She suddenly saw that Rémi wasn't alone. She nodded in response to Pascale's greeting, then looked at Rémi attentively. Pascale noticed that he seemed tense and nervous and wondered why.

Andrea sat down in an armchair.

"You look like a pair of conspirators," she said slowly. "What fascinating subject were you discussing when I came in?"

Rémi put out his cigarette in an ashtray.

"We were talking about Etienne," he answered gruffly.

A mocking laugh filled the room.

"Then it wasn't a very pleasant conversation. Pascale had another chance to see his indifference last night." She held up her little dog. "It's easier to solicit affection from an animal. This one is a darling and he adores me." She kissed her pet on the nose and went on: "Well, Rémi, what have you decided about

Etienne? I think it's cruel to make Pascale put up with his viciousness any longer. Since the 'big sister' experiment has failed, have you decided to take Irène's advice and find a good institution for disturbed children?"

Rémi didn't answer. Although Andrea hadn't spoken to her, Pascale couldn't help protesting.

"An institution like that wouldn't give Etienne what he needs. Let him have playmates and I'm sure he'll stop thinking up ways to misbehave."

Andrea yawned.

"Let's not talk about that again. It bores me. For the time being, you can do whatever you like with Etienne. But Rémi will have to make a decision about him very soon."

Pascale was struck by the look of weariness in Rémi's eyes.

"The decision is up to Pascale," he said. "I can't expect her to go on trying to accomplish something with Etienne if she feels it's beyond her strength. And I already owe her a debt of gratitude that—"

"You don't owe me any gratitude," interrupted Pascale, "and the idea of giving up has never crossed my mind. Just give me more freedom in playing the part of a 'big sister,' as Andrea put it. Tell Clotilde that she can stop taking care of Etienne. I want to do everything for him myself, as if he were. . . ."

She blushed and fell silent. Rémi smiled at her affectionately.

"As if he were your own son," he finished gently.

Pascale's embarrassment increased. She looked at Andrea, afraid she might have unintentionally offended her. But the latter seemed to have no interest in the conversation. Humming a popular song to herself, she was lovingly combing her little dog's fur.

"Listen to me, Andrea," Rémi said without raising his voice, but in a peremptory tone that made her stop humming.

"I'm all ears, darling."

"From now on, only Pascale will take care of Etienne. And if she wants to take him to a public park, or invite children to play with him here, that's exactly what she'll do."

"Irène is afraid of contagious diseases in public parks," objected Andrea, still combing her dog's fur. "I hear that many of the children who go to Trianon Park are catching measles these days."

"Do you think there are no contagious diseases in boarding schools?" Rémi asked sarcastically. "If there are measles in Trianon Park, Etienne can play in the Luxembourg Gardens. Serge will drive him there. I want you to see to it that no one in this house criticizes Pascale's decisions. Do you hear me, Andrea?"

"Yes, of course I hear you. There, look how pretty my Youki is! He's the prettiest dog in the world! Have you noticed how shiny his fur has become since I started giving him vitamins?"

She laughed lightheartedly, stood up and hugged the little dog against her chest. Her beautiful but expressionless violet eyes turned to Pascale.

For the first time, Pascale wondered if that capricious young woman, who seemed to have no maternal feeling for her son, was entirely responsible for her acts. *Maybe the whole trouble with Etienne is that he has a mentally deranged mother,* she thought with discouragement. She pushed aside the idea a moment later, but it left her with a feeling of uneasiness.

PASCALE DECIDED to take Etienne with her to Paris one day.

At first she had a personal reason for her decision: she wanted to see Lambert again, since she was afraid her abrupt rejection of his proposal might have hurt him. His studio was near the Luxembourg Gardens, so it would be easy for him to come talk with her awhile. But when she was about to call him, she changed her mind. The idea seemed almost a betrayal of Rémi's confidence in her. Since she had been given complete charge of Etienne, she owed him her undivided attention.

So far, respecting Irène's orders, she had taken Etienne only for short walks in the park of the Versailles Palace. Irène had told her that he had slipped away from two other governesses and that it had taken long hours of searching to find him. So Pascale had watched him carefully and made him stay close to her. But she didn't like such precautions and noticed that whenever something was forbidden to Etienne, he became determined to do it. The more barriers were put up around him, the more he wanted to break them down. So she decided to be more flexible and avoid provocative prohibitions.

Rémi had already told Serge he wanted to be driven to his office in Paris that afternoon. He offered to take Pascale and Etienne with him. Etienne seldom went anywhere with his father. He was so proud that he behaved perfectly all during the trip.

He and Pascale climbed out of the car at the little park next to the Hôtel des Invalides, where they were to remain till Serge came back for them. Rémi went on to his office on the Rue de l'Université.

Pascale sat on a bench in the shade, gave Etienne the toy truck she had brought for him and left him free to play.

"You can do whatever you like here," she explained carefully, "but the traffic on the street is very dangerous. I know I can trust you not to go outside the park."

His expression told her she had adopted the right approach. While keeping a constant watch on him, she pretended to be absorbed in her book. The park was small enough to make it easy not to lose sight of him.

The only children there were younger than Etienne. He didn't take advantage of the freedom Pascale had given him: he played with his truck, never straying very far away from the bench where she was sitting. Finally he asked for his afternoon snack.

While he was eating his sandwiches, his curiosity was aroused by a boy of seven or eight who had just come into the park, wearing patched trousers and a faded blue shirt. He was followed by a dirty little dog of uncertain breed. The boy kept kicking a pebble in front of him as if it were a soccer ball, concentrating all his attention on it and ignoring everything around him. His thin, undernourished face was crowned by a mass of tousled blond hair.

Etienne went toward him and deliberately stopped in front of him.

"What are you playing?"

The other boy looked at him in surprise, then said rather disdainfully, "I'm not playing. I'm dribbling."

"Oh," said Etienne, puzzled.

They were both silent for a moment.

"What's your name?"

"Claude. What's yours?"

"Etienne."

"You live around here?"

"No, I live in Versailles."

A look of wonder came into Claude's eyes. To him, Versailles meant only the royal palace described in his book of French history.

Etienne pointed to the little dog, who had calmly sat down a few feet away.

"Is he yours?"

"No, I found him this morning behind the garbage cans. He's a stray and looks like he hasn't been getting much to eat. Feel how skinny he is."

The two boys bent down and felt the dog's bony spine. He had the general shape of a basset hound and his head looked a little like a fox terrier's. His wooly, reddish brown fur was matted with dirt. His yellow eyes were bright with intelligence.

Etienne broke off a piece of bread from his sandwich and held it out to him. It disappeared with amazing speed. Piece by piece, he fed the dog his whole sandwich. Then, remembering that he still had two cookies left from his snack, he ran over to Pascale's bench and came back with them, holding them up triumphantly.

The dog gulped them down, then pressed his head against Etienne's leg and looked up at him, his eyes begging for love as much as food. Etienne patted him with a thoughtful expression.

"He likes you already," Claude said without bitterness. "You ought to keep him. I can't. We're not allowed to have any animals in our building."

"If nobody takes him, what will happen to him?"

"He'll be put in the pound."

"What's that?"

"It's a kind of jail for dogs . . . or else he'll be run over by a car."

Etienne's eyes opened wide with horror. He was gripped by an oppressive feeling that he knew only too well.

"No!" he said fiercely. "I won't let him die! Wait for me."

He picked up the dog and hurried to Pascale, who had been watching the scene from her bench.

Claude saw him talk with her for a few moments, then come back.

"He'll be safe now! I can keep him!"

They sat down on the grass, the dog huddled against his new master. Claude looked at Pascale and smiled sadly.

"Your mother's very nice," he said quietly.

Etienne didn't feel any need to correct him.

"What's *your* mother like?" he asked.

"She died when I was little. I have a stepmother now. Sometimes I wish I didn't."

"What's a stepmother?"

"Don't you know *anything?* A stepmother yells all the time and hits you."

They were still talking together when Pascale saw Serge stop the car at the curb, near the entrance to the park. She went over to them.

"It's time to go home, Etienne . . . just a minute, I forgot to bring your truck. It's behind the bench."

Followed by Claude, Etienne went to find it. As they were about to leave, he handed the truck, his favorite toy, to his new friend.

"Here, take it. You'll see how it works. The doors open and you can take the wheels off."

Claude stared at it and whistled with admiration.

"It's a real beauty! Thanks a lot!" He patted the dog one last time. "What name are you going to give him?"

Etienne thought for a few seconds, then his face brightened.

"Since I met him in a park, I think I'll call him Parky. It's a good name."

"Yes, I like it," Claude replied approvingly.

Pascale anxiously wondered if the happiness shining in Etienne's eyes would be enough to make his parents accept the stray dog she had rashly told him he could keep.

But she was sure of one thing: her experiment in giving Etienne more freedom had proven he wasn't as bad as his family thought. A really vicious child wouldn't have shown such sensitivity. His family considered him quarrelsome and brutal with other children; yet he had been perfectly sociable with Claude. She was puzzled by the great difference between his behavior in the park and the way he usually acted at home.

Maybe he feels misjudged, she thought, *and rebels by showing exactly the faults he's accused of having.* That explanation seemed plausible to her, but didn't completely satisfy her. Besides, she was wary of all theorizing, even her own.

Serge was waiting on the sidewalk next to the car. When he saw the wretched-looking dog trotting beside Etienne he stared in surprise but said nothing.

Etienne picked up the dog and proudly introduced him to Serge: "This is Parky. I'm taking him home to live with us."

Serge gave Pascale a disapproving look. She suddenly felt very uneasy.

On the Rue de l'Université, Rémi quickly got into the back seat of the car, beside Pascale. In the front seat, Etienne didn't look around. Rémi reached out and playfully rumpled his hair.

"Did you have a good time in the park?"

Etienne didn't answer. He hugged Parky against his chest, as if he were afraid that treasure would soon be taken away from him.

Rémi leaned forward to see what he was holding.

His eyes widened in amazement. He turned to give Pascale a questioning look and saw apprehension in her face.

"It was a stray dog," she explained contritely.

Rémi gave her a smile full of life and warmth and took her hand in his to give her the reassurance she obviously needed. She was deeply touched by that gesture of affectionate confidence. Her fears dissipated and all at once she realized that nothing mattered to her but Rémi's approval.

She gently withdrew her hand. But the friendly complicity between them left a glow of joy in her heart.

"Can I keep my dog?" Etienne asked pleadingly.

Rémi patted his cheek.

"Yes, if you promise to behave better from now on."

"He will," said Pascale.

Etienne lifted Parky like a glorious trophy, turned around and put him down on the floor of the car in front of Rémi and Pascale. Kneeling, with his chin on the back of the seat, he looked at them with an expression of tenderness that neither had ever seen on his face before. Then a smile put two dimples in his cheeks.

"I've got a terrific father," he said with conviction.

Chapter 6

The grass along the bridle path was still damp from the rain that had fallen during the night. Above the two riders, a vault of foliage rustled gently in the morning breeze. The air was cool and fragrant.

Pascale and Rémi had let their horses slow to a walk after trotting for several miles. When they came to a place where the path wound down into a little valley and disappeared into a patch of mist, they turned to the right. Although the new path was narrower, they went on riding side by side.

Wearing blue jeans and a white cotton jumper, Pascale felt the warm caress of the sun on her back. When she leaned forward to stroke the horse's neck, she saw that Rémi had done the same thing at the same time. They looked at each other and smiled.

"You work miracles, Pascale," he said in his deep resonant voice. "Did you know that your mare has the reputation of throwing her riders and galloping away from them? But she's been perfectly docile with you. I watched you while you were getting acquainted with her. There seemed to be a kind of mysterious understanding between you, and she was as gentle as a plow horse. You must have some sort of divine grace that lets you bring out the best in people and animals."

"Is simply loving them a divine grace?" she asked, laughing.

A gust of wind blew away some of the silvery wisps of fog that still clung to the branches. The sun ignited reddish highlights in Pascale's hair. Her face had the delicate freshness of a newly blooming flower. Sitting straight in the saddle, but without stiffness, she gave the impression that every fiber of her body was closely following the movements of her horse.

Rémi looked at her for a few seconds, then bowed his head; his features contracted as though from sudden pain. She didn't notice.

"So you let me ride a bad-tempered horse without warning me!" she said playfully. "What if she'd thrown me off and broken all my bones?"

Surprised not to hear him answer, she looked up and saw him staring ahead vacantly, a lingering sadness on his face. Her happiness was abruptly dulled. She was afraid something she had said might have stirred up a secret source of bitterness in him.

The image of Andrea came into her mind. *I've never seen a man so obsessed with his wife,* she thought. *He's madly in love with her, yet they seem to take spiteful pleasure in making each other suffer.*

Andrea had apparently changed her mind about going to Deauville. For two days she had gone with Pascale and Rémi on their morning ride. She was an excellent rider but she treated her horse brutally and was so reckless that she sometimes endangered her companions.

On the third morning, tired of waiting for her in the car long after they were supposed to leave, Rémi had sent Pascale to find out what was keeping her. Pascale had stopped in front of the open doorway of Andrea's bedroom. Standing before a large mirror, wearing pale-green pajamas with an outrageously low neckline, Andrea seemed fascinated by her own reflection.

Hearing Pascale's voice, she turned and looked at her with strangely empty eyes. Long moments went by before she finally realized what was expected of her. She yawned and stretched, then laughed.

"You're absolutely tireless, Pascale! Do you really want to go galloping through the woods again this morning? I've had more than enough of it. From now on, you and Rémi will have to get along without me."

Pascale went back to the car.

"Andrea says she's too tired to go riding this morning," she said to Rémi.

He didn't answer but she saw a shadow pass over his face. She was hesitant to enter the car. Even though Andrea hadn't seemed to mind at all, she felt she shouldn't go riding with Rémi alone. People were always ready to gossip, and several times she had noticed how careful he was never to draw attention to his private life.

As a pretext for not going with him, she pointed out that they would be starting much later than on the other mornings.

"What of it?" he said sharply. "There's no reason why you have to stay here. Etienne usually sleeps late, and he won't be alone when he wakes up. Irène, Clotilde or Berthe can certainly manage to take care of him till you get back."

He smiled. "Just for once, Pascale, why don't you

do as you please, without worrying about what people will think?"

And so every morning for the past two weeks they had left the house at seven o'clock, gone to the riding club and taken a long ride in the forest.

They shared those outings in a spirit of relaxed companionship. Pascale discovered what her heart had been longing for: a sensitivity equal to her own and an affinity of tastes and ideas. The growing friendship between them was strengthened by her love for Etienne. Sooner or later their conversation always turned to the subject of his behavior, which still puzzled them.

Pascale had taken him back to the little park near the Hôtel des Invalides. Claude had been there again, but he had said he would soon be leaving for a summer camp. Etienne spent several happy afternoons in the park.

Then, when Claude had left, his attitude changed. He met other children and treated them so badly that Pascale had to take him to another park. At the Champ-de-Mars she met the same disappointment. An indignant mother came to her to complain that Etienne had savagely attacked her son. After that, she stopped taking him out. Now and then he still showed a surge of affection for her, but immediately afterward he always became more unpleasant than ever, as if to wipe away the memory of his brief weakness.

Only his love for Parky remained constant. The little dog now shared his whole life. His influence was sometimes annoying to Pascale because he seemed to control Etienne's acts even when absent. If Etienne refused to do something, it was because Parky had told him not to.

Rémi was the only one in the family who appreciated Pascale's efforts to change Etienne. Neither Andrea nor Irène believed it would ever be possible to improve him.

As she rode along in the sunlight, Pascale remembered something Irène had said to her: "No amount of understanding or patience will have any effect on him. He's a pathological case, as I've always told Rémi. Only a psychiatrist could find out what the trouble is, whether it's sickness or . . . heredity."

Irène had almost whispered this last word and hadn't commented on it, but her expression had clearly shown that she had a definite opinion on the subject.

"You seem worried, Pascale. What are you thinking about?"

Rémi's voice jolted her out of her reverie.

"Etienne, of course," she answered. Then, after a short silence, she said hesitantly, "Are you sure you've eliminated all the possibilities that might complicate the problem with him? What I mean is . . . do you think he might have some . . . deep-seated disorder, something that. . . ."

He looked at her so sharply she felt herself blushing.

"Let's stop here," he said. "Your question is too serious to be answered lightly. A little farther on, the trail becomes rocky and we'll have to give all our attention to guiding our horses."

They both dismounted. Pascale leaned against the side of her horse, still holding the reins. Rémi stepped close to her and put his hand on her shoulder.

"You were referring to the possibility of a hereditary defect, weren't you? I'm sure you didn't think of it all by yourself. Who suggested the idea to you?"

"Well, I—"

"Answer me with the frankness I like so much in you. It was Irène, wasn't it?"

She nodded.

"What did she insinuate?" he asked.

His voice had taken on a certain hardness. She felt his hand tremble on her shoulder but she looked straight into his eyes.

"She didn't insinuate anything. She'd like to have a psychiatrist examine Etienne and check on anything that might influence his character, whether it's illness or a heredity problem."

He saw she was telling the truth and his face relaxed. The pressure of his hand became friendlier.

"I mistrust psychiatrists too much to turn Etienne over to one of them. They live in a strange world that warps their minds so much that they tend to regard everyone as a case that falls within their specialty. Etienne has never been seriously ill, and I can assure you there's no reason to believe he may have a hereditary defect."

He said these last words forcefully, but with a look of weariness on his face. *He seems to be trying to convince himself,* thought Pascale. She couldn't forget Andrea's strange instability.

"But since you're a future doctor," he went on bitterly, "you agree with Irène, don't you?"

"No," she answered without hesitation. "You asked me what I was thinking about and I told you, but I don't share Irène's opinion."

He had leaned toward her, as if to concentrate on the meaning of her words. The sun was shining directly on his face and she saw each detail of it with striking clarity. She realized that his handsomeness came less from the regularity of his features than from their expression of deep, intense life. Intelligence, kindness and energy radiated from his face like an inner light. But that light seemed veiled by the weary expression that accentuated the lines around his mouth.

She felt she understood the reasons for his anxiety. *He's always thinking of Andrea, with her dazzling beauty and her magnificent body. And he's in despair because the woman he loves so passionately keeps slipping away from him. But he also knows she's not completely responsible for her acts, and he doesn't want anyone else to discover that painful secret. The slightest suspicion would tarnish the image that he keeps in his heart in spite of everything.*

"What's *your* opinion?" he asked.

She looked up with a start. She had become so absorbed in her own thoughts that she had lost the thread of the conversation. As she was trying to recall it, he misinterpreted her silence.

"Is what you've discovered in Etienne so serious that you don't want to tell me about it?" he said in a faltering voice.

All the friendship she felt for him appeared in her face. There was nothing she could do to make him stop tormenting himself about Andrea, but she could at least try to relieve his anxiety over what Irène had said.

"In my opinion, the trouble with Etienne," she said with calm firmness, "is that he's been raised as if he were a little prince, according to the principle that a child shouldn't take part in family life till he's learned to behave properly in society. But what Etienne needs most is love. In a less aristocratic household, he'd eat his meals with his parents, go out with them and find them always there when he wanted to talk with them. They'd give him the warmth he needs. I think part of the problem with him comes from the fact that he doesn't have enough of that warmth."

It had taken great courage for her to say this. To soften the effect of it, she added with a disarming smile, "To him, you and Andrea are as wonderful as characters in a fairy tale, but just as inaccessible, too."

He remained silent. His face was impenetrable.

"I have a feeling I won't be able to convince you," she said, "but remember how happy and outgoing he was when we came back from Paris in the car with you."

"Yes, I remember . . . but why doesn't he always respond to me that way? He seems to have much more affection for Parky then he does for me. What's your explanation for that?"

"I don't have one. I've been trying to understand it, but. . . ."

They were both silent for a few moments. Pascale had let go of her mare's reins. The two horses were now grazing a short distance away. Rémi had put his hands behind his back and was distractedly watching a woodpecker hammering at the rough trunk of an oak.

He suddenly took Pascale by the arm and pointed to the top of a tree.

"Look at that squirrel," he said softly.

She looked intently but saw only a reddish form flash between two branches. They stood still, captivated by the peaceful beauty of the forest. The sunlight shining through the leaves turned the bark of a birch to silver, inflamed the red hawthorn berries and transformed the last dewdrops into glittering jewels.

Pascale was blissful for no apparent reason, except perhaps a wonderful harmony between her and the vibrant joy that emanated from the forest. She lived those moments with such precious intensity that she wished she could make them last forever. She stood perfectly still, for fear of breaking the spell, until Rémi's hand quivered slightly on her arm.

Suddenly the woodpecker flew away with a loud rustling of wings. The mare started and abruptly raised her head. The enchantment had ceased.

"It's late," sighed Pascale, looking at her watch.

Rémi emerged from his reverie. A radiantly youthful smile brightened his face when his eyes met hers.

"Yes, we'd better start back soon," he said. "But first, let me tell you how grateful I am for everything you've given me in the past two weeks."

She raised her eyebrows questioningly. He went over to the horses and led them back before explaining: "During our morning rides, I've been like a thirsty traveler drinking the cool, clear water of a spring. Your sensitivity and understanding have meant more to me than I can say. With you, I can forget my work and my worries. Even the problems with Etienne don't seem insoluble any more, thanks to your insight. You always seem to know exactly what he needs. You'd be a perfect mother, Pascale."

"I couldn't take much credit for it, since I love children so much," she replied laughing. "But why are you talking as if this ride were going to be the last? We won't be leaving till a week from now."

He helped her into the saddle, then mounted his own horse and they set off along the trail again at a trot.

"I have to leave today for a business trip to Brussels," he said. "I expect to stay a few days, then go on to Geneva. Andrea will meet me there and we'll spend the rest of the summer in Switzerland, as we have planned."

Pascale's mare stumbled and she had to concentrate all her attention on the trail. The forest suddenly lost its festivity. She sighed. The joy in her heart had strangely vanished.

"I won't see you again till we come back," Rémi went on, "and by then I hope to find Etienne completely transformed. I've been thinking of what you said about him. We'll try an experiment. I'll be home till two o'clock today. Etienne will have lunch with us, and we'll make it a kind of family reunion. If the results show your theory is right, he'll stop having his meals alone in the pantry. There, what do you think of my idea?"

"I think it's excellent," said Pascale.

Chapter 7

Andrea and Irène were a constant mystery to Pascale. She could never predict their reactions. They would fly into a rage when she expected them to be pleased, then show nothing but indifference when she was dreading an outburst of anger.

She had assumed there would be a stormy scene when Etienne came home with Parky. Rémi had broken the news to Andrea and Irène. Pascale didn't know how he had gone about it, but to her amazement they seemed to accept the little dog without protest. During the day he played in an enclosure near the garage that had once served as a kennel, and at night he slept in the bathroom between Etienne's and Pascale's rooms.

Knowing Irène's views on child-rearing, Pascale was sure she would never accept the idea of letting Etienne have his meals with the adults. But even if she did give in, it seemed unlikely that the "family reunion" would take place as Rémi had planned , since it turned out that Andrea intended to go to Paris that morning for a fitting at her dressmaker's, then meet some friends at a restaurant for lunch. Pascale couldn't believe she would change her plans when Rémi asked her to stay home and take part in the experiment he wanted to try.

Once again, Pascale's expectations were wrong. At a quarter past twelve the whole Sévrier family sat down to lunch in the dining room. Not only had Andrea agreed to change her plans, but there was no sign of resentment on her smiling face. Irène's expression was no colder than usual. Rémi seemed relaxed.

Sitting on either side of Andrea were two guests. One of them was Henri Reynat, a plump, jovial businessman who had come to pay a friendly visit while his wife and children were spending their vacation at Royan. The other was René Marchand, one of Rémi's assistants. Rémi had invited him to stay for lunch when he came to bring him some important papers.

Rémi sat opposite them, between Pascale and Irène, and kept up a lively conversation.

At one end of the table, Etienne stoically put up with the blazer, white shirt and bow tie that he had been asked to wear in spite of the heat. Irène had always told him that only grownups could eat in the dining room, so he was filled with pride at having been suddenly given that privilege. He tried especially hard to watch his manners because he sensed that his mother and his aunt were hostile to Pascale. From overhearing a conversation between her and Irène, he knew she was responsible for his being allowed to eat with the grownups.

"It's ridiculous to give him the privileges of an

adolescent when he's only six," Irène had said angrily. "You'll see. His behavior will prove I'm right."

He had no intention of proving that Aunt Irène was right. She would use it as an excuse for being even more unpleasant to Pascale.

At first he was intimidated by that solemn dining room, where he had hardly ever been before. He felt out of place when he looked at the long, dazzlingly white table with silverware, dishes, plates and glittering crystal lined up on it like soldiers on parade. Even Serge and Clotilde, who did the serving, no longer seemed to be the same people he saw every day. They had been turned into robots dressed in white and black who did their work with haughty dignity.

No use expecting any help from them. They wouldn't cut his meat for him, or remind him that he shouldn't drink with food in his mouth. He would have to face his responsibilities alone and make sure he didn't forget anything he had been taught.

His determination to act properly made him awkward. As he was eating a slice of cantaloupe with a spoon, it slipped off his plate and onto the tablecloth. Luckily his father was so engrossed in conversation with his two friends that he didn't notice it. His mother never noticed anything. Only Irène and Pascale reacted: Irène by giving him a murderous look, Pascale by discreetly calling Serge over to her.

"Give Etienne the silverware he usually eats with," she requested quietly. "That spoon is much too big for him."

At the same time she put her hand on Etienne's arm reassuringly, to let him know there was no need to be upset over such a trifling incident. He thanked her with one of the fleeting smiles he sometimes gave her. They were always more wonderful to her than the first flower of spring.

She wasn't worried. Etienne had decided to behave himself. She could see it clearly in his face. But she doubted that the results of the experiment would be very good. This wasn't the kind of family gathering that would give Etienne the warmth he needed. To Andrea and Rémi, who were used to large dinner parties, this lunch at home with seven people might seem an intimate gathering, but to Pascale, who remembered the casual good humor of her family's meals, it had the stiff, strained atmosphere of an official banquet. *I'm sure he can't feel any contact with his parents,* she thought. *This insecurity is the exact opposite of what I wanted.*

She took part in the general conversation but did her best to keep Etienne from being embarrassed. As she was helping him cut his meat, she was sharply reprimanded by Andrea.

"Please let him fend for himself, Pascale. How do you expect him to prove he's ready to eat with adults if you keep helping him?"

There was a strong tinge of rancor in her voice, and when Pascale looked at her she saw such hostility in her eyes that she was secretly alarmed. The fact that Irène treated her with thinly disguised dislike didn't upset her. Rémi had warned her: "Don't let Irène intimidate you. She'll be disagreeable to you no matter what you do. It's her character and there's nothing to be done about it." But since Andrea was usually friendly to her, she was surprised and hurt by this sudden animosity.

There was an inevitable silence. Then Rémi said with calm self-assurance, "Etienne has already given us plenty of proof that he's ready to eat with adults." He leaned toward his son and winked at him affectionately. "Keep up the good work, I'm proud of you."

Etienne's face turned red but Pascale couldn't tell if it was from embarrassment or pride.

Irène felt called upon to explain to the guests: "This is the first time he's ever eaten at our table. It was Pascale's idea. Personally, I don't think it's right to let such a young child take part in adults' conversation."

"He hasn't been taking part in it very much," Henri Reynat said affably. "I've never seen such a well-behaved young man. My children make a lot more noise than he does!"

"But do you let them eat at your table?" asked Andrea.

Reynat laughed good-naturedly.

"Certainly not! We wouldn't be able to hear ourselves think! They're absolutely unbearable. My wife isn't as lucky as you: she's never found a governess who can keep them under control."

"Pascale isn't a governess," said Rémi, smiling. "She's a friend who's been kind enough to help us during her summer vacation. I don't know what we'd have done without her. Every year Etienne goes to our country house in Les Landes, but this year Irène is tired and Andrea is going to Geneva with me. I'll be there several weeks for the Jacquemain trial. . . . Have you spent much time in Switzerland?"

To spare Pascale the embarrassment of being the focus of attention he had adroitly turned the conversation to the subject of Switzerland.

Pascale scarcely listened. She was trying to find an explanation for the resentment that had been so obvious in Andrea's eyes.

She must hold me responsible because she had to change her plans today, and she's probably annoyed with me for making her put up with Etienne during lunch. She has no motherly feelings at all. But why didn't she refuse when

Rémi told her what he wanted her to do? Till now, she's always done exactly as she pleased, whether he liked it or not. Why did she give in this time?

She nervously crumbled a piece of bread while Serge changed the plates. She felt ill at ease, as if everyone were looking at her, yet she knew no one was paying any attention to her. The others were discussing the vacation attractions of the Swiss lakes.

She turned her head when Clotilde brought a tray of cheeses. A moment later she realized the reason for her uneasiness. Andrea was glaring at her. Her face quickly became as expressionless as usual, but not before Pascale had seen the hatred in her violet eyes. That discovery chilled her to the heart, then anxiety began rising in her like a tide.

She remembered what Rémi had said just before they went into the dining room, while she was alone with him for a moment in the hall: "In Brussels I'll be staying at the Royal. Don't hesitate to call me if you have any kind of trouble, or if something that seems odd happens here. I'll see to it that the hotel knows where to reach me immediately if I'm not there."

At the time, she hadn't attached much importance to these words, but she now sensed a hidden meaning in them: they were a warning. Her anxiety increased still more.

"Will you be staying in Geneva the whole time you're in Switzerland?" Reynat asked Andrea.

"Yes," she answered. "Rémi's business affairs will keep him in the city. And since our stay there will probably be quite tiring, I'll go with Pascale and Etienne to Estello, our country house in Les Landes, and have a few days' rest before leaving for Geneva."

Rémi stiffened and Pascale couldn't help raising her eyebrows in surprise. This was the first time Andrea had said anything about such an intention. Till now it had been agreed that she would go to Geneva on the day Pascale and Etienne left for Estello.

"I didn't know you'd decided to do that," said Rémi. "I thought you were bored to tears at Estello. . . . Estello is a real hermitage," he explained to his guests. "There are no neighbors except for the farmers who live more than a quarter of an hour's walk from the house. The nearest beach is at Vieux Boucau, and it's not a very social place."

He spoke in a natural tone but, looking at him from the side, Pascale sensed his agitation from the nervous twitch of a muscle in his jaw. He seemed irritated by Andrea's latest whim.

Pascale secretly admired Andrea's cleverness in not announcing her intention till she was certain Rémi wouldn't oppose it. He was leaving as soon as lunch was over, so he would have no chance to be alone with her and he wouldn't object to such a seemingly normal plan in front of his guests.

"The peace and quiet will do me good. Sometimes we all need to take a pause in the hectic lives we lead," she said, leaning toward the guests as though asking for their agreement.

Rémi had difficulty keeping himself under control.

"We've been invited to gatherings in Geneva at the beginning of our stay, as you well know. We can't miss them."

"*I'll* miss them," she said with a bland smile. "I'll stay at Estello for a week at the most, long enough to relax. Irène will go there tomorrow, by train, to organize the house."

She addressed herself to the guests: "Only the gardener and his wife stay here during summer vacation; we let the other servants take time off. At Estello we hire local servants. Irène takes care of such matters very well. I believe Pascale, Etienne and I can leave in four days. Serge will drive us."

Rémi made no objection. His face was calm but hard. Irène mentioned a story she had recently read in a newspaper and the conversation turned to current events.

No one but Pascale paid any attention to Etienne. During a moment of silence toward the end of the meal he looked at his mother and asked, "Are you going to take Youki to Estello with you?"

"Of course," she answered with a little laugh.

"And what about Parky?"

"Children mustn't talk at the table," Irène said sharply.

Etienne ignored her.

"Parky wants to come too."

"Don't worry," said Rémi, "there's enough room for two dogs at Estello."

Andrea gave a forced smile, as if the discussion bored her; then she stood up and said to the guests, "We'll go into the drawing room for coffee. I'm sorry to rush you like this, but Rémi has to be in Brussels by six o'clock. What is it, Berthe?" she asked the second maid, who had just come in.

"A telephone call for Pascale."

"For me?" exclaimed Pascale, surprised.

She hadn't given her address to friends because she didn't want them calling her in a house that wasn't hers. Only Lambert and her mother knew the Sévriers' number. And since her mother hadn't written to her for several days, she suddenly felt worried.

"Do you know who's calling?" she asked Berthe.

"He said his name was Lambert."

Andrea quickly looked around as she was leading

her guests into the drawing room next door. Only Irène noticed her agitation. She immediately pointed toward a window and drew the others' attention to the dark clouds gathering in the sky.

"You can take the call in my study," Rémi said to Pascale as she was walking toward the telephone in the entrance hall. "Push the red button and you'll cut off all the other extensions in the house."

"HELLO, LAMBERT?"

"Pascale, at last!" exclaimed a voice from the telephone. "You took long enough to answer! What were you doing?"

"I came as soon as the maid told me you were calling. Is anything wrong?"

"I just wanted to talk to you."

"My mother isn't sick, is she?"

"No. Or at least I hope not. I haven't seen her since you left."

"Too much work?"

"I've been working like a maniac. I'm doing a theater set for a play that will open in September. It takes a lot of time but it's fascinating."

"I'm glad you've found your inspiration again," Pascale said with a touch of irony but no bitterness.

She knew that Lambert's enthusiasms usually coincided with a new infatuation. She also knew that till now he had never had the slightest interest in designing theater sets. She concluded that in spite of the great passion he claimed to have for her, he had fallen for a woman who was connected with the theater in one way or another.

She smiled indulgently. *How fickle he is!* she thought. *It's lucky I didn't take that letter of his seriously.*

"What do you mean by that?" he asked a little aggressively.

"Just what I said: I'm glad you've found your inspiration again."

"You said it as if you thought. . . . Look, don't get any wrong ideas in that suspicious head of yours. I've been thinking about you constantly, from the first day of our separation to the last. Because this is the last day we'll be apart. You're going to quit your job and come back to Paris, and then—"

"And then we'll go camping together in Brittany?" she finished mockingly. "Don't count on it, Lamb!"

"Pascale!"

"Please don't shout."

"Listen to me, Pascale. You have to leave Versailles immediately."

"Is that an order?"

"Yes. No. . . . Let's say it's something my love for you makes me strongly advise you to do."

She answered with a ripple of laughter.

"Pascale!" he roared. "If you don't promise to leave there today, I swear I'll come and bring you back myself!"

She was silent for a moment. Her left hand toyed with the seventeenth-century lacquered box on Rémi's desk. She snapped it shut.

"There's no point in talking about it any more. I agreed to take care of a child till the end of summer and I have no reason to go back on my word. You can take someone else camping with you in Brittany."

"Forget about that! I don't care about camping in Brittany, or anywhere else! Listen to me—"

"No. I don't like to listen to people who keep shouting. I have sensitive ears."

"Please, Pascale! You're in danger there. Don't stay with that family another hour."

This time he had spoken without raising his voice, but with such firm conviction that Pascale couldn't help feeling a twinge of anxiety.

"Explain what you mean," she said.

"I can't. Someone may be listening on another phone. There are several extensions in that house, aren't there?"

"Yes, but the one I'm using now is cut off from the others."

"Where are you?"

"In Monsieur Sévrier's study."

"What are you doing in his study?" Lambert asked with sudden anger. "You're not his secretary! Is he with you now?"

Her anxiety was swept away by irritation. She began to suspect that the "danger" Lambert had spoken of was something he had invented in an effort to get her away from Versailles because his plans were upset by her stay there.

"I don't think that's any concern of yours," she said curtly.

"I just want to know if anyone else can hear what you say."

She sighed with exasperation.

"There's no one in the room with me, and the doors are closed. So tell me about the terrible thing that will happen to me if I stay here."

"I can't talk about it on the phone. Trust me. I know for certain that you're in danger, but that's all I can tell you now."

"You read too many detective stories," she said sarcastically. "Have a good vacation—without me, of course, because—"

"You *must* listen to me, Pascale! It's very serious!"

"I've listened too much already. Don't worry, I'm perfectly safe here, but you'll have your wish anyway: you want me to leave Versailles as soon as possible, and it so happens that we're leaving for Les Landes in less than an hour. No, I don't know the address. I'll write you when I get there. Goodbye, Lamb."

She hung up.

That little lie will make him leave me in peace, she thought. *I don't know what's wrong with him; with his lively imagination, he should have come up with something better than a mysterious danger that he can't explain to me on the phone.*

She shrugged as if to dismiss the whole thing from her mind, but a moment later she was annoyed with herself when she realized that she still had a lingering trace of uneasiness.

Chapter 8

The threatening storm burst early in the afternoon. The wind drove sheets of water against the whole west side of the house. In the drawing room, a window had been left open and rain poured in through it until a good part of the rug was sopping wet. When Irène discovered it she was furious and her recriminations put all the servants in a bad mood.

Pascale soon realized that things were going to be more difficult for her with Rémi away. Shortly after he left for Brussels, Andrea and Irène started an argument with her on the first pretext that came to hand: Etienne's nap.

Now that he was six, Etienne felt he was too old to go to bed after lunch. Rémi and Pascale agreed. For nearly a month, his afternoon nap had been replaced with a rest period during which Pascale read stories to him.

But Andrea now decreed that it was a mistake to let

him form such a habit, because after Pascale was gone there would be no one with the patience to read to him for an hour every day. Irène forcefully approved of her sister's reasoning. Pascale pointed out that after she was gone Etienne would start school, so the problem wouldn't even arise. She was ignored.

Irène undressed Etienne and put him to bed, much against his will. His pleas, shouts and threats had no effect on her. And when he tearfully asked for Parky, she told him a nasty little dog like that belonged outside and not in a bedroom.

He finally closed his eyes and seemed to fall asleep. But half an hour later, when the storm was still raging outside, Pascale came across him in the hall. Water streamed from his hair and pajamas and he was clutching a very wet dog against his chest.

"Parky was afraid of the thunder," he said.

Pascale made no comment. She quickly took the two of them to the bathroom. After putting Parky in the bathtub so he could shake himself without wetting the floor, she undressed Etienne, rubbed him vigorously with a towel and brought him dry pajamas.

He said nothing but he kept giving her furtive looks, trying to judge how angry she was. When Irène scolded him, he enjoyed seeing her eyes flash and her cheeks turn red. If he succeeded in making her stammer with fury, he gleefully savored his victory.

With Pascale it was different. He talked back to her only as a way of asserting his independence. And when he saw sadness mingled with the affection in her eyes, a hard little lump came into his throat. He knew it would go away if he cried but he didn't want it to go away. It was part of the secret suffering he kept inside himself and never showed to anyone. He always stiffened his will and called on all his pride to keep himself from throwing his arms around Pascale.

"Why are you frowning?" he asked when she had put him to bed again and tucked him in.

"Because your mother and your aunt will be sad when they find out what you did. You may catch a cold from getting so wet."

He shrugged.

"They don't care if I catch a cold or not, and anyway they won't know what I did."

"They'll see that Parky isn't in his kennel."

That hadn't occurred to him. He doubted that his escapade would cause any sadness to his mother and his aunt, but he was sure he would be punished for it. He was suddenly chilled by the thought that he might not be allowed to take Parky to Estello with him. He had twice heard Aunt Irène threaten to put "that dirty mutt" in the pound and he knew she was quite capable of doing it. If she did, he would go to live with Parky in the pound. And if they wouldn't let a boy stay in a jail for dogs, he would kill himself. It wasn't hard. He had already tried it once when he felt too unhappy. All you had to do was put your head under water and take a deep breath. . . . No, that wasn't the best way. You felt too sick when you woke up. He would do what Youli had done: run in front of a car.

He began trembling as he always did when that horrible memory came back to him. He hadn't wanted Youli to die, and yet it had been his fault. He had forgotten to close the front door. Youli had gone out of the house, through the open gate and into the street. As soon as he saw what had happened, Etienne had run after him, but just as he was getting close enough to catch him. . . .

To drive away the image he pressed his fists against

his eyes so hard that bright sparks danced behind his eyelids. It did no good. Through the sparks he still saw Youli's crushed little body. He silently struggled against that nightmare till something struck him on the chest and made him start.

After being dried by Pascale, Parky had pushed open the bathroom door, run into his master's bedroom and jumped up on him. Etienne's anguish instantly vanished. He hugged his friend, pressing his face against the damp, strong-smelling fur. In exchange for that tender gesture he received a wet kiss on the nose and two on the neck. They were both silent, knowing that the slightest sound would bring Pascale out of her room and put an end to Parky's visit.

Suddenly the little dog raised his head and pricked up his ears. Then he jumped to the floor and lay down with his nose between his front paws.

The door from the hall opened. Etienne recognized his aunt and quickly closed his eyes.

Irène tiptoed into the room. She had just had a violent argument with Andrea and was still far from calm. The shutters of the room were closed. When her eyes had adjusted to the semidarkness, she saw the dog.

Sensing disaster, Parky flattened himself against the floor as much as he could. But Irène knew how to control herself. She stopped a few feet from him, restraining a strong urge to kick him out of the room. She looked at the two accomplices with hatred, then quietly went through the bathroom and into Pascale's room.

A QUARTER OF AN HOUR LATER, Pascale leaned her forehead against the windowpane and looked out at the roses shaken by the storm. She felt dejected, but not because of the harsh things Irène had said to her. Since she had protected Etienne by taking the blame for bringing Parky into the house, the reprimand she had received from Irène was no more than she expected.

Her dejection had deeper roots. She was profoundly depressed by the indifference and even hostility that surrounded Etienne. She couldn't understand how Andrea could be so lacking in maternal feeling. Ever since she had known her, she had seen her kiss Etienne only once, on the day he had nearly drowned. But she had to admit he had shown no reaction to that kiss.

Can it be that she and Irène have simply been discouraged by his coldness? she wondered. *No, that's not enough to explain their resentment against him. They reject him from their lives. They regard him as an obstacle, a constant annoyance.*

She was suddenly appalled by the realization of how much harder her task was going to be now that she had to face it alone. Rémi wanted her to act as an "older sister" to Etienne. It was his support that had enabled her to play that part till now. He had even succeeded in making Irène's tyranny more bearable. Pascale could always count on him for the reassurance she needed when one of her experiments with Etienne ended in failure. Now there was no one to guide, protect and encourage her.

With Rémi gone, she would no longer have the warmth and sympathy that had made her feel as if she were almost one of the family. She was now only a stranger who was tolerated because she was useful. A terrible feeling of isolation swept over her when she considered the days that lay ahead. She remembered riding through the sunny forest and was suddenly surprised by the depth of her feeling as she pictured Rémi riding beside her: his strong hands holding the reins, his energetic face, the tenderness that came into his eyes when he spoke of his son. . . .

This was the first time the thought of a friend had ever aroused emotions in her. She was ashamed and quickly repressed them. Nothing in Rémi's attitude toward her justified what she had just felt for him. Furthermore he was married and he loved his wife, in his own tormented way. It wasn't in Pascale's nature to abandon herself to a hopeless romantic passion. And she had great self-discipline where strong principles were concerned.

She sighed wearily, went over to her desk, opened one of the medical books she had brought with her and began studying it. At first it was difficult to concentrate but the remedy finally took effect and the image of Rémi faded from her mind.

A DISCREET KNOCK on the hall door made her look up.

"Yes?"

"Here's your tea," said Clotilde, coming into the room.

"Five o'clock already!" Pascale exclaimed after glancing at her watch. "And Etienne is still asleep!"

"I can wake him up and dress him if you want me to," offered Clotilde. "I have to wait for Mademoiselle Irène to come back and tell me what else she wants in her suitcase. She's gone shopping with Madame and won't be back for another half hour. What a time we've had with her today! She's never been more disagreeable. I'm glad she's leaving tomorrow. Do you want me to wake Etienne up? What an idea to put him to bed after lunch! A big boy like him—"

Pascale interrupted her, smiling.

"No thanks, I'll take care of him myself. You can take this chance to get a little rest."

"All right, I think I will. But if you need anything, just let me know."

"Thank you."

Clotilde hesitated, went to make sure the bathroom doors were closed, then said softly, so that Etienne couldn't hear, "Monsieur is going to Brussels, isn't he?"

"Yes. Why?"

"I heard on the radio that north of here the storm was even worse. It caused a lot of accidents on the road to Brussels. I hope nothing has happened to him."

"I hope so too."

Pascale cleared her throat because she had scarcely recognized her own voice. The idea that Rémi might have had an accident caused her physical pain.

When she went into Etienne's room, the first thing she did was to open the shutters. The rain and wind had stopped. In the park, the leaves were dripping. On the street beyond, cars rolled along the wet pavement with a swishing sound. Before closing the window she breathed in the cool air saturated with the smell of damp earth. Even though the sky looked threatening, she decided to take Etienne out for a while.

She turned and couldn't hold back an exclamation of surprise. Etienne was not only up, but had already dressed himself and was now sitting in his little armchair, waiting patiently with Parky at his feet. He had even made his bed, though not very neatly. On the blue satin bedspread was the big beach bag that

Pascale usually carried when she took him out. It was swollen like a balloon.

Seeing her look at it, he explained: "I put in my bear, my pajamas, a jacket, a raincoat and Parky's cushion."

"But why have you started packing so soon? We're not leaving till Tuesday."

He stood up, looked her straight in the eyes and said firmly, "The three of us are going to Brussels to be with papa. It's not hard. All we have to do is take the train. Parky told me all about it. He knows everything."

Pascale knew she was in for a battle. When Etienne announced that Parky had told him something, it usually meant he would insist on his decision with fierce determination. It was better to try to reason with him, rather than beginning with a hard and fast refusal.

She sat down on the edge of the bed.

"Your father is in Brussels for his work, not to enjoy himself. I'm afraid we'd be a bother to him if we went there. And what would your mother say when she saw you were gone?"

He stepped closer to her.

"*You're* my mother."

She took him on her lap. To her surprise, he didn't resist, although he sat rather stiffly.

"You mustn't say that," she protested. "I love you as much as if you were my little boy, but you know very well that—"

"You don't want me?"

"What a question, Etienne! You belong to your mother and she's the one you should love most of all. I'm only here to help her."

"Help her do what?"

Pascale sighed. The conversation was becoming

difficult. The idea of substituting herself for Etienne's real mother seemed unscrupulous to her, yet she had so much more maternal feeling than Andrea! From the depths of her being she hoped her warm tenderness would penetrate him and melt the hardness that still remained in him.

He didn't give her time to think of an answer. In a gesture of abandon that moved her deeply, he pressed his head against her and began talking in a low voice.

"I'm not mama's little boy. I'm not anybody's little boy. Aunt Irène told me so one day when she was angry. So I can choose you if I want to. Parky chose *me*, and I said yes right away, because I knew he was unhappy. I want you to be my mother."

These words were the fruit of Pascale's love and devotion, but Etienne hadn't been able to say them till his heart was stirred when she protected him from Irène's anger and took the blame for something he had done.

He bowed his head and blushed to the roots of his hair, ashamed at having bared his deepest feelings and afraid she might make fun of him.

She was speechless. She was beginning to understand at last. The base of the problem was something Irène had once said, probably in a fit of uncontrollable rage. What had it been? Pascale didn't know, but the exact words didn't matter. What mattered was the meaning Etienne gave to them. He was "nobody's little boy." His aggressiveness was a reaction against the despair of feeling unwanted and alone in a hostile world.

She felt sudden joy at the thought of being able to reassure Rémi by sharing his discovery with him. She would write to him the next day.

But first she had to reassure Etienne. She put her finger under his chin and lifted his face. Big tears were rolling down his red cheeks. He felt he was even unhappier than Parky had been, since he interpreted Pascale's silence as meaning she didn't want him.

"You have parents and a home," she said, "so you can't compare yourself to Parky: he was a homeless dog. But if you have a little extra room in your heart for me, I'll be glad to be your second mother."

Like a ray of sunshine after a rain, a smile full of life brightened his face. He wiped away his tears with the back of his hand and awkwardly kissed her on the cheek.

"I didn't mean I wanted two mothers," he said as if he was explaining something that should have been obvious to her. "Papa was already in my heart, and now you are. I chose you both because you're the ones I love. And I don't want Aunt Irène to make you feel bad any more, so we'll take a train tonight and go to papa."

Pascale was at a loss for a moment, then she leaned down and patted Parky.

"He's still a little thin," she said. "A vacation at Estello would do him more good than a stay in a pound."

"A pound? I don't want him to stay in a pound!"

"I'm afraid there's no way out of it," she said in a falsely resigned tone. "Brussels is in Belgium. The guards at the border don't let any dogs go through. They keep them in a pound till their owners are ready to leave the country."

"How can we keep them from getting Parky?"

"The most sensible thing for us to do is to go to Estello instead of Brussels."

Etienne wasn't convinced.

"Aunt Irène is mean to you, and you know Parky and Youki will fight during the trip."

"Your Aunt Irène is sometimes strict, but she's not

mean. Anyway, we'll be out of the house most of the time at Estello. And don't worry about the trip. You can hold Parky on your lap. There won't be any trouble."

He thought for a long time, frowning. Finally his face relaxed and she knew she had won.

"When we get to Estello," he said, "we'll go see the Nogares. Aunt Irène doesn't like them but I always go there with papa."

"Who are the Nogares?"

"They're farmers. There's César and his wife, Lydia. They take care of the animals and work in the woods. They have two big daughters named Emmanuelle and Blanche. They help Aunt Irène at Estello. Their grandmother sits in the sun all the time. She's very nice and sometimes she tells me stories. Her name is Pascaline—" He stopped short, struck by a similarity that had never occurred to him before. "Pascaline's name is almost the same as yours. But you're even nicer than she is. Nobody in the whole world is as nice as you!"

Chapter 9

When they hurried back from their walk because the rain had begun falling again, they found suitcases piled up in the entrance hall. There were others on the second-floor landing. Clotilde came hurrying out of Andrea's room and jostled Pascale without even noticing.

Pascale was puzzled. She didn't see why Irène's departure should cause so much agitation or require so much baggage. Something must have happened to make Irène change her plans. Pascale's thoughts immediately turned to Rémi and the image of an accident came back to haunt her.

Etienne counted the suitcases on the landing.

"One, two, three, four, five . . . all that for Aunt Irène? Why is she taking so many things with her?"

Pascale was too upset to respond. With her eyes closed, she felt anxiety rising inside her despite her efforts to stop it.

A door slammed on the third floor. She opened her eyes and called to Etienne, who was hopping along the hall on one foot.

Berthe came down the stairs, carrying a big suitcase and wearing her best clothes.

Trembling with apprehension, Pascale walked toward her.

"Why all this commotion?" she asked. "What happened while we were out?"

Berthe looked up and down the hall. When she had made sure all the doors were closed, she said softly, "It's one of Mademoiselle Irène's sudden ideas, only this one is in our favor. That doesn't happen very often. All of us except the gardener and his wife are going on vacation sooner than we thought. Serge and the cook have already left. Clotilde will leave as soon as she's finished packing. I'm hurrying to get out of here before the wind changes. With such peculiar people, you never know. . . . Well, goodbye. I hope you enjoy your stay in the country."

Pascale forced herself to answer politely. Her anxiety had given way to amazement. She felt slightly dazed.

She finally became aware that Etienne was doing a frenzied dance around the suitcases.

"We're leaving! We're leaving! We're leaving!" he shouted joyfully at the top of his lungs.

He was answered by Youki's barking from Andrea's room.

Andrea suddenly opened her door.

"What an uproar! You can't hear yourself think in this house! Pascale, will you please make that child be quiet? Just look how nervous he's made Youki! The poor little darling will be trembling for hours."

With her dog under her arm she came out to the

middle of the landing. She was wearing a simple, dark green dress and, for once, low-heeled shoes. Pascale was surprised. At seven o'clock in the evening, Andrea was usually dressed much more elegantly, ready to go out.

She ordered Etienne to go to his room. He scowled and took his time about obeying, then rebelliously slammed his door.

Andrea sighed with exasperation.

"Just give him a few more years and he'll be a full-fledged juvenile delinquent!"

"Let's not exaggerate," said Irène's voice.

Pascale turned around. Silently as always, Irène had come up behind them. Her expression was odd. Her thin lips were stretched into a smile that was meant to be friendly, but the look she gave her sister was hostile and the redness in her cheeks showed restrained anger.

"Etienne may still be a little unruly," she went on, "but surely he won't turn out to be a juvenile delinquent. Don't underestimate the good influence Pascale has had on him. . . . Have you told her about our change of plan?"

"I was waiting for you, Irène," announced Andrea.

The gentleness of her tone contrasted with the animosity in her eyes. Pascale, who had always seen the two sisters closely united, was surprised by the antagonism she sensed between them now. It made her uneasy, as if she had discovered an embarrassing secret. And Irène's unaccustomed compliment aroused her suspicions.

"I just came back from a walk with Etienne and I don't know what's been happening," she said to break the silence. "Are we all going to leave tonight?"

Irène's smile broadened.

"As far as you're concerned, Pascale," she said, "the only change is that you'll travel by train. You'll still leave on Tuesday, with Etienne. We've had to change our original plan because Serge has left. He got a telegram this afternoon telling him that his mother is seriously ill. We told him he could begin his vacation early and go to her immediately. To avoid making the other servants jealous, we told them they could also leave early, except for the gardener and his wife. They always stay here while we're away on summer vacation.

"As you know, we have only two cars. Rémi drove the Rolls-Royce to Brussels. Andrea and I decided it would be better for us to leave in the Mercedes this evening. Les Landes is more than a ten-hour drive from here. It's south of Bordeaux, down near the Spanish border. By traveling all night we'll avoid heavy traffic for most of the trip. If we take turns driving, each of us will be able to get some sleep in the car."

"What train shall we take?" asked Pascale.

"I've already made reservations for you and written down the details on a sheet of paper that you'll find on Rémi's desk, along with an envelope containing money for tickets. You'll take the train at the Austerlitz station in Paris and get off at Dax. I'll meet you there and drive you to Estello."

At first this plan seemed perfectly logical to Pascale. It was normal that Andrea wanted to accompany her sister and preferred to drive rather than take the train. But then Pascale began to feel there was something in Irène's reasoning that didn't ring true. What was it? She didn't know, but she couldn't help the vague misgivings that crept over her for the rest of the evening.

She ate a light supper with Andrea and Irène.

Etienne was sent to bed early as punishment for having been insolent to his aunt. The tension between the two sisters was so strong that Pascale felt as if one wrong word might set off an explosion. She was relieved when they drove away in the white Mercedes shortly after nine o'clock.

PASCALE COULDN'T SLEEP THAT NIGHT. The uneasiness that had been gnawing at her ever since supper became a strong anxiety she was powerless to control.

She kept turning Irène's words over in her mind until she finally realized what was wrong, and she remembered Lambert's warning. It was Irène's explanation of Serge's abrupt departure. If he had really received an urgent telegram calling him to his mother's bedside, he would have told the other servants about it. Yet Berthe had said only, "Serge and the cook already left."

It now seemed clear to Pascale that Irène had sent the servants away for quite different reasons. And why did she and Etienne have to spend four days alone in the house when they could have left for Estello that evening? She wasn't at all reassured by the presence of the gardener and his wife, who lived in a little cottage near the entrance gate. The house was filled with valuable objects. If a burglar came into the park by climbing over the wall, then forced open one of the windows at the back of the house, the couple in the cottage would be completely unaware of it.

Her nerves were on edge and the slightest cracking in the woodwork sent a cold chill along her spine. She suddenly had a thought that made her leap out of bed, trembling. Lambert was mistaken. She wasn't the one who was in danger: it was Etienne, the only child of a rich and prominent couple.

As she pulled on her bathrobe she tried to remember the details of kidnappings she had read about in the newspapers. The more she thought about it, the more her anxiety seemed justified. Through a strange combination of circumstances, the isolated, poorly protected house provided ideal conditions for a kidnapping.

After making sure Etienne was sleeping peacefully in his bed and the shutters of his room were tightly closed, she decided to sit up the rest of the night. She opened both doors to the bathroom and began her vigil in an armchair, ready to leap up at the slightest alarm.

She was sorry she had taken Lambert's warning so lightly. What had he found out? She thought of calling him and demanding an explanation, but then hesitated because she would then have to admit she had told him a lie. Furthermore her pride rebelled at the idea of asking for his help after she had so confidently rejected it.

She felt a little reassured when she remembered what Rémi had said to her before leaving: "In Brussels I'll be staying at the Royal. Don't hesitate to call me if you have any kind of trouble, or if something happens that seems odd to you. I'll see to it that the hotel knows where to reach me immediately if I'm not there."

So far she hadn't really had any trouble and she doubted that he would see anything odd in what had happened. During supper Andrea had told her Rémi had called from Brussels and expressed approval of Irène's decision, so he apparently saw no reason why Pascale and Etienne shouldn't stay alone in the house. She wouldn't call him, but the knowledge that she *could* was a relief. It was the life buoy she clung to when her anxiety became overwhelming.

It was also a distraction, because in spite of herself,

the thought of Rémi always filled her with longing.

She hadn't been aware of her feelings until after he had left. Trying to analyze them she recalled the long, friendly conversations during those morning rides, the shared efforts in trying to understand Etienne, and her joy each time the sadness in Rémi's eyes was dispelled by an improvement in his son's behavior.

Was it only pride in her success that had made her so happy?

She examined the question without flinching and tried to find the answer in the depths of her heart.

Her pride was mingled with a more complex feeling that had escaped her awareness at the time. It had grown without her realizing it and now was solidly rooted in her soul. It wasn't the maudlin passion of a young woman addicted to romantic daydreams. Her unhappiness told her it was something much stronger and deeper.

She was in love with Rémi, and that love now filled her whole life.

This realization took complete possession of her, blotting out the fears that had been preying on her mind since the beginning of the night. A rush of shame made her forehead feel hot. She leaned forward and buried her face between her hands.

Am I incapable of controlling my feelings? she wondered. *Because I'd never been in love, I thought I was stronger and more sensible than most of my friends. How wrong I was! And has my affection for Etienne partly grown out of my impossible love for Rémi?*

She again questioned herself mercilessly. It became clear to her that even if she had never met Rémi, she would still have the same feelings for Etienne. That certainty soothed her tormented conscience.

She tried to calm herself by making resolutions for

the future. Perhaps she couldn't be held accountable for the love that had taken her unawares, but from now on she had to repress it so completely that no one would ever suspect its existence. If it left her with an incurable wound, she would keep her feelings to herself.

She sat up straight, then leaned her head against the back of the chair. Outside, the rain was falling more heavily. Its monotonous patter rose above the occasional small sounds inside the house. In the bathroom, Parky woke up, saw the open door, slipped into Etienne's room and lay down beside his bed.

A clock struck three.

Somewhere in Pascale's room a piece of furniture cracked. She awoke with a start, annoyed with herself for having dozed off. She stood up, turned on a light and went to make sure Etienne was covered. For a few moments she stood listening to his regular breathing. She felt bewildered and unhappy, but ready to give her life for Rémi's son if need be.

Her fear had vanished. She began shivering, but only because she was cold.

AT NOON the telephone in the entrance hall rang just as Pascale was coming back from a walk with Etienne. She picked up the receiver.

"Hello."

"Is that you, Pascale?"

She immediately recognized Irène's voice.

"Yes, it is. Did you have a good trip?"

Irène ignored this question and came straight to the point.

"I'm calling to ask you to postpone leaving Versailles. I'm sorry, but you can't come to Estello till a week from now. I'll need that time to put everything in order and feel completely recovered. Change your train reservations to next Saturday. Do you hear me?"

"Yes, I hear you very clearly," replied Pascale, disconcerted. "But if you're tired, I'll be glad to help you. It seems to me that I'd be more useful if—"

"Is Etienne with you?" interrupted Irène.

"Yes."

"Then invent some reason to make him go away."

Pascale turned around and sent Etienne to wash his hands in the pantry.

There was a short silence, then Irène said, "I'm going to tell you the truth, Pascale, because I think I can trust you not to panic. Last night Andrea and I had an accident in the car. A doctor treated us at the scene of the accident; luckily we weren't seriously injured, but we'll need several days of complete rest to recover from the shock. I'm calling from a village hotel, so there's no need to worry about us. If we'd been injured we'd be in a hospital. It is important for you to delay your departure."

"But are you sure you'll get the care you need at a village hotel? Don't you want me to come there? That would be—"

"No," Irène said brusquely. "There's a doctor in the village."

"Where did the accident happen?"

"Not far from here. . . ."

Irène's voice was nearly drowned out by a burst of background noise on the telephone line. Pascale thought she heard, "I'm calling from Bellac."

"Isn't that in Haute-Vienne?" she asked.

"Why should we be in Haute-Vienne?" Irène's voice was perfectly audible now. "We're near Bordeaux."

"Does Rémi know what happened?"

"Yes, I've already called him. But I hid part of the truth from him. I was afraid he'd be too upset if I told him Andrea had been in an accident, so I just said the car had broken down and I'd sprained my ankle."

"Does he know that Etienne and I won't leave for another week?"

"Of course," Irène replied curtly. Then her tone became friendlier: "We'll be expecting you on Saturday. You'll have to take a taxi from the station at Dax, since our car is unusable. In the meantime I'll call you every morning to let you know how we're feeling. Don't worry, we'll be all right. Goodbye, Pascale."

"Goodbye."

She hung up, making an effort to keep her hand from trembling. She was dismayed by the news of the accident and the prospect of spending a whole week of sleepless nights in that deserted house. Although the thought of asking them embarrassed her, perhaps she should prevail upon the gardener and his wife to sleep in the main house.

She wondered if Andrea had been more seriously injured than Irène had led her to believe. Since the car was beyond repair, the accident must have been quite serious. The more she thought about it, the more she became convinced that Irène had hidden part of the truth from her as well as from Rémi.

She would have liked to share her apprehensions with someone. For a moment she thought of calling Rémi's friend Henri Reynat, who had come to lunch the day before, but she was held back by the fear of being indiscreet.

She went to the kitchen, where the gardener and his wife were eating lunch. Etienne, who had been talking with them instead of washing his hands, was sent to the bathroom.

As soon as he had closed the door behind him,

Pascale began telling them her story in a voice that faltered with emotion. But the expressions of astonishment that greeted each new revelation convinced Pascale she was doing the right thing.

Chapter 10

"The whole thing sounds fishy to me," said Reine, the gardener's wife. "If I were you, I'd call Monsieur right away."

Gaston, her husband, had just finished drinking a glass of wine. He wiped his mustache and said, "So would I. It sounds fishy to me too. And coming from Mademoiselle Irène, it's not surprising. Lying is as natural to her as breathing. Reine is right. Since you know where to get in touch with Monsieur, you'd better call him."

Until his death five years earlier, when they had come to work for Rémi, they had faithfully served Rémi's father for forty years. They were both in their seventies, but still vigorous and alert. Rémi treated them with great affection and they were completely devoted to him. Since they lived in their own little cottage, apart from the other servants, Pascale had seldom talked with them before although she had noticed that they always looked sullen when Irène gave them orders.

"You know as well as I do how Madame and her sister feel about Etienne," said Reine. "He gets on their nerves and they do everything they can to avoid having him around." She was silent for a moment, looking at Pascale's tormented face. "You shouldn't put much stock in what Mademoiselle Irène told you, take my word for it. She may have made up that story about an accident for reasons of her own. You'd better tell Monsieur."

"But he already knows about it," protested Pascale. "She called him this morning."

"How do you know?" asked Gaston. "She told you she did, but that doesn't make it true."

Pascale lifted her hands and let them fall helplessly. She thought of what Rémi had told her. This time something "odd" really had happened. But did she have a right to oppose Irène by calling him?

Reine found the right argument to overcome her hesitation.

"I know it's not true, and I'll tell you why," she said. "If he knew you were staying here alone with Etienne, he'd have already called to ask how the two of you were doing. The best thing will be for me to call him and tell him what's going on. That way, Mademoiselle Irène can't blame you. What's the name of his hotel in Brussels?"

"The Royal."

PASCALE HAD JUST FINISHED straightening up Etienne's room when Reine opened the door and asked her to come out into the hall.

"Monsieur is leaving Brussels right away," she whispered. "He'll be here this afternoon. I was right:

he didn't know anything. The poor man was terribly upset when I told him!"

"SENDING ALL THE SERVANTS AWAY less than four hours after I left, leaving you alone here with a six-year-old child—I suppose it all seemed perfectly normal to you! What would it have taken to disturb you? Had you decided there was no need to call me unless the house burned down or Etienne was kidnapped?"

"Oh!"

Rémi's eyes softened when he saw the look of painful remorse on Pascale's face. He stopped pacing the floor of his study and sat down at his desk.

Twenty minutes earlier his Rolls-Royce had stopped in front of the house with a crunch of gravel. Etienne had run out to meet him and hugged him exuberantly.

"Pack your things and Etienne's," Rémi had said gruffly to Pascale. "We're leaving in an hour. Ask Reine to help you. Come to my study when you're ready."

She had never heard him speak so harshly to her, or seen such an implacable expression in his eyes.

And now, in his study, she had great difficulty holding back her tears as she tried to justify her conduct.

"Andrea told me you knew what Irène had decided and approved of it. I saw no reason to bother you."

He frowned without answering. He opened a drawer, took out a map and spread it on the desk in front of him.

"Where did Irène say she was calling from?"

Pascale felt more wretched than ever.

"I'm afraid I didn't understand the name," she confessed. "It sounded like Bellac to me, but that couldn't be right because she said they were near Bordeaux. I'm sorry. I should have asked her again, but I was so upset that—"

"It doesn't matter," said Rémi, pushing the map away from him. "She was probably lying anyway. I can easily find out. I have a friend who's a newspaperman in Bordeaux. I'm going to call him and ask him to check with the police in all the nearby towns to find out if that car was involved in an accident last night. If the answer is what I think it is, he'll be making phone calls for quite a while!"

His bitter laugh only accentuated the pain that showed in his face. Pascale felt as if she could read his thoughts. She was sure he was tormented by jealousy. She turned her head away to dry her eyes while he was calling his friend in Bordeaux.

As soon as he had hung up he began pacing the floor, as if incapable of sitting still. With his hands behind his back and his head thrust forward, he seemed to have forgotten Pascale's presence.

Five minutes later the telephone rang. She watched him as he picked it up. His jaws were clenched so tightly that the muscles bulged and for a fraction of a second she wondered if he would be able to speak.

"Hello, Grisel? Yes . . . I see. . . . Thank you, I'm very grateful. . . . Yes, that's true . . . thanks again. Goodbye."

He put down the receiver and kept his hand on it for a long time; his sagging shoulders seemed to bear the weight of the world's sorrows. Finally he drew himself erect.

His eyes met Pascale's and in answer to her silent question he said, "Their car went off the road and turned over near Belin, about thirty miles south of Bordeaux. The dog was killed but Andrea and Irène weren't seriously hurt. I don't understand why they weren't killed too: the speedometer was blocked by the impact and it showed that the car was going almost ninety miles an hour."

"Belin?" murmured Pascale. "That must be the name I confused with Bellac."

Rémi bit his lower lip. He was silent for a few moments, absorbed in his thoughts. Then he asked abruptly, "What time did Irène say the accident happened?"

"She didn't give me any specific time. She just said 'last night.' "

"And did she give the name of the hotel she was in?"

"No, and I didn't think to ask."

"It's not important. I'll find out. . . . Are you ready? I want to leave very soon."

She nodded.

"Yes, I'm ready, but you seem terribly tired. Wouldn't it be better to rest awhile before starting such a long drive? And there can't be many hotels in Belin, so why not ask the operator for their numbers and call them? It won't take long to find the right one. That way you'll be reassured before you start."

"What makes you think I'd be reassured?"

He spoke more gently this time, giving her a long, scrutinizing look. She blushed but didn't turn her eyes away.

"If they were seriously hurt, they wouldn't be in a hotel,"she insisted. "The mere fact that they're not in a hospital is reassuring."

"Is that what Irène told you?" he asked with heavy sarcasm.

Pascale didn't understand why he still seemed suspicious of Irène, since her report of the accident had turned out to be true. Maybe his morbid jealousy was so strong that it made him see deceit where none existed.

"Your honesty is one of the things I like most about you, Pascale," he said, stepping close to her and affectionately putting his hands on her shoulders. "You have such a noble heart that you can't see treachery even when it stares you in the face. And Irène is treachery personified. Do you know when the accident happened? At ten-thirty this morning. And at eleven o'clock she called me in Brussels to tell me that all four of you—that's right, *all four of you*—had arrived safely at Estello."

"But . . . but why?" stammered Pascale.

"To make sure I wouldn't call here. She didn't want me to know that you and Etienne were alone in the house. As for her lie to you about the time of the accident, that was to hide something else. What? I'd rather not think about it. Sometimes I guess too well. Let's leave now. I won't be able to clear up the mystery till we're in Belin. There's no use calling to say we're coming. It would only give Irène time to invent another lie."

ETIENNE'S BEHAVIOR THAT AFTERNOON was astounding. As the gardener and his wife were putting suitcases into the trunk of the Rolls-Royce he threw his arms around them and then, after kissing their wrinkled cheeks, he bent down and patted the cat he had once thrown into the basin of the fountain. The animal purred contentedly, sensing through some mysterious instinct that there was no longer anything to fear from him.

As he was about to get into the car with Parky, Etienne took on his most winsome expression and asked to be allowed to sit in the front seat. Rémi refused. Pascale was going to sit there, he said. But, understanding Etienne's needs, she interceded for him.

"He's so happy to be with you again," she said. "Let him sit there till it gets dark, then he can lie down on the back seat and go to sleep."

"That way, Pascale and I can both have a turn," reasoned Etienne.

Rémi gave in with a smile.

The rain had stopped and the wind had dried the road. Etienne chattered happily as they rode along. Rémi answered him with apparent cheerfulness but Pascale knew the effort he was making to hide his real feelings.

"You've transformed Etienne," he said, adjusting the rearview mirror so that he could see her in it. "I hardly recognize him now. He's like a little ray of sunshine."

"And Pascale is a *big* ray of sunshine!" Etienne said enthusiastically.

Rémi laughed. And this time his laughter rang true.

When they has passed Chartres, Etienne's exuberance began to fade.He seemed to be sinking into a kind of torpor. Finally he stopped talking altogether.

"Don't fall asleep," Rémi said to him. "We're going to stop for dinner before long."

Etienne sat up straight. His attention was soon riveted on two motorcycle policemen far ahead of them, going in the same direction.

Pascale studied the map. She had located Belin on it and wondered why Andrea and Irène preferred to recover from their shock in a modest hotel there, rather than going on to their comfortable country house, since it was only forty miles away.

Rémi's thoughts were following a similar course.

He was haunted by the strange circumstances of the accident: ninety miles an hour on the heavily traveled highway from Bordeaux to Bayonne, at ten-thirty on a Saturday morning, when weekend traffic must have been at its height. Andrea and Irène were both experienced drivers. What could have made them take such a foolish chance?

The three travelers had a late dinner in a restaurant near Vendôme. They still had nearly 300 miles to go. Etienne's eyelids were drooping sleepily. Rémi drank two cups of strong coffee.

He stood up and looked at his watch.

"We should get to Belin by two in the morning."

He had stopped putting up a cheerful front for Etienne's benefit. He was pale and anxiety had deepened the lines around his mouth.

"Do you want me to drive for a while?" asked Pascale. "I have a license. My mother has an old Chevrolet that she sometimes lets me use. I think I can handle your car."

He smiled at her and shook his head.

"You need rest more than I do, Pascale. I'm sure you didn't sleep a wink last night. You and Etienne are both ready for a nap. Look at him. He hasn't even finished his dessert."

When they returned to the car, Etienne stretched out on the back seat and Pascale covered him with the blanket she had brought. He fell asleep less than a minute after they started off along the road again.

"Does the open window bother you?" Rémi asked Pascale.

She looked at him. His strong profile seemed softer in the dim glow of the dashboard lights.

"No, I'm not cold."

Fatigue weighed heavily on her body but her mind

was still clear. She abandoned herself to a blissful feeling of well-being. Her present happiness seemed as fleeting as the flashes of light that briefly caught the shapes and colors of the trees beside the road. She wished she could hold back the elusive minutes that kept slipping into the past. Through the workings of chance, she was again with the man she loved. She knew that all his words and gestures would be indelibly imprinted on her mind. She felt joyful at being so close to him and imagined herself leaning over to touch him. But her love was akin to worship. It didn't show itself in provocative movements or languid poses. She kept it enclosed in her most secret depths. She realized all too well that it would soon become a source of pain but she was too weary to struggle against it now.

She looked up with a start when she heard his voice again.

"Can you tell me by what miracle you've dissolved that discontentment in Etienne? Less than two weeks ago he was disagreeable, unsociable and thoroughly unbearable. You've turned him into a happy, sensitive and loving child. Are you a magician, Pascale?"

"Not at all," she said, laughing, "and the result isn't perfect, far from it. Etienne still lets his temper get the best of him and he loves to do things he's been told not to."

"I'm not thinking of faults like that; they're common to all children his age. I'm thinking of the hardness that used to be a basic part of his character. It's mysteriously disappeared. Remember our long discussions about it? You were convinced that what was good in him was blocked by a closed door. I'd like to know how you succeeded in opening that door."

Pascale nearly answered, "I gave him what he

lacked, love." But that would have been unfair to Rémi. For a time she had inwardly accused him of cold-heartedness toward Etienne, but she had long since changed her mind on that score.

"I can't take any credit for it," she said. "I knew something was making him unhappy but it was only by chance that I discovered what it was, and then I was able to cure him of it. He'd somehow gotten it into his head that he was no one's child."

The car abruptly swerved to the left. Pascale stared in surprise but saw nothing in the road.

"Who gave him such a ridiculous idea?" Rémi said hoarsely.

"It was his own doing. He misinterpreted something Irène said, and then, with the help of his imagination, he convinced himself that no one loved him or wanted him. From then on, his anxiety must have caused serious emotional disturbance. He became uncommunicative, vindictive, filled with hatred, and he reacted aggressively against children and even animals who seemed to be loved and cherished, because he saw them as having what he lacked."

Rémi let long minutes go by before asking, "How did you free him from his anxiety?"

"I'm not sure I've really made him realize his mistake," she said hesitantly. "To put his heart at peace. I had to offer to be a second mother to him. Andrea may consider that unscrupulous, but I had no choice."

He didn't answer. She looked at him, feeling a little disappointment. In the dim light his face seemed even more tense. He peered straight ahead at the road, insensitive to the chilly air coming in through the open window and seemingly oblivious to Pascale's presence. *He disapproved of what I did,* she thought sadly.

She now felt cold. She turned up the collar of her jacket. For a time she let her thoughts wander over the whole problem of Etienne. She noticed distractedly that Rémi was driving much faster than the speed limit. Then she leaned back against the seat and fell asleep.

Chapter 11

She was awakened by a restrained "woof" from Parky. It took her a few moments to realize where she was. The car was parked on a street lined with elm trees. The stars were dimmed by the first faint glow of dawn. Houses were beginning to emerge from the darkness. A gray owl that had been perched on the hood of the car flew away. Parky growled again.

She sat up and saw that she had been covered with a wool blanket. At the other end of the seat, Rémi was asleep with his arms crossed on the steering wheel.

He was awakened by her movement when she leaned forward to look at the dashboard clock. He rubbed his eyes and pushed the hair back from his forehead; then he too peered at the dashboard.

"Four o'clock," he said softly. He turned toward her and a friendly smile relaxed his face. "What a life I impose on you, poor Pascale! You'd be so much better off in your bed! I thought I could hold out till we got to

Belin, but several times I nearly dozed off while I was driving. It was too dangerous to go on without taking a short nap. I thought I'd sleep for twenty minutes or so but it turned out to be more than three hours."

"And I slept even longer," said Pascale, smiling back at him. "I feel completely rested now—and embarrassed at having taken the whole blanket."

Behind them, Etienne was curled up on the seat, still sound asleep.

"He's as comfortable as if he were in his bed at home," Rémi remarked.

"Where are we?"

"About an hour from Bordeaux. Allowing for the time it will take us to go through the city, we've got nearly two more hours of driving ahead of us. But it's probably better this way. I doubt if the hotel keeper would have given me a very friendly welcome in the middle of the night."

He opened the door to let Parky get out and stretch his legs. Chilly air poured into the car. Pascale spread her blanket over Etienne's feet. Parky hopped back inside.

"Off we go again," said Rémi.

He was silent for the rest of the trip.

THE TIME SEEMED TO PASS so slowly. For fear of being indiscreet, Pascale hadn't offered to accompany Rémi. The car was parked a short distance from the hotel. After waiting more than half an hour for him to come back, she wondered whether he would decide to spend the day in that little town or go on to Estello.

She got out of the car and walked a few steps along the street. Yellow sunlight illuminated the rooftops of the houses. She looked at the hotel into which Rémi had gone wearing such a grim expression. All the shutters were still closed. She wondered which of them enclosed Andrea's and Irène's room.

A maid carrying a shopping bag emerged from the hotel and crossed the street.

Pascale went up to her.

"How are the two women who came to your hotel yesterday, after their accident?"

The maid stared at her in puzzlement. The question seemed to baffle her. Finally a glimmer of understanding appeared in her eyes.

"You must mean the woman in room three. The doctor brought her yesterday. But there was no one with her."

Pascale felt her legs weaken.

"Then where *is* the other woman? In a hospital?"

"Are you talking about the accident with the Mercedes?"

Pascale nodded.

"There was nobody in the car but the old lady and her little dog. The dog was killed. She certainly wasn't afraid to drive fast—you should have seen what the car looked like after—"

"Thank you," interrupted Pascale, who had just seen Rémi walking rapidly away from the hotel.

She hurried toward him. All traces of anxiety had vanished from his face. His expression now showed nothing but implacable determination. She took him by the arm and forced him to stop.

"Please tell me what happened. Where's Andrea?"

"At Estello, I suppose. We're going there right now. Is Etienne awake?"

"Not yet. How's Irène?"

That name ignited a blaze of anger in his dark eyes.

"She's all right. No one ever died of a sprained ankle. She'll join us in a few days. Let's hurry."

He suddenly became aware of how upset Pascale looked. His face softened. He put his arm under hers and began leading her toward the hotel.

"Forgive me, Pascale, I was forgetting that it's early in the morning and you spent the night on a car seat. Come in and have something hot to drink. We'll leave when you're feeling better."

She nearly refused, but then changed her mind. It would be better if Rémi had a chance to calm down a little before starting to drive again. She didn't understand very well what had happened but she assumed his anger resulted from some escapade of Andrea's.

A maid brought them two cups of hot coffee and put a basket of stale rolls in front of them. Rémi was obviously impatient to leave. Instead of calming him, this delay was only making him more nervous. Pascale stood up as soon as she had finished her coffee.

A few minutes later they were back on the straight, flat road with its border of pines. Their rough trunks had been turned pink by the glow of the morning sun. It was a beautiful sight, and Pascale remarked on it. Rémi seemed not to have heard her. He was driving dangerously fast.

"I'll leave you with the Nogares. They're a family of farmers who live about a quarter of a mile from the house," he explained, after glancing at Etienne sleeping in the back seat.

He wants to take Andrea by surprise, thought Pascale. *Is he so obsessed by his jealousy that he doesn't care about making a fool of himself?*

She looked at him out of the corner of her eye. He suddenly seemed an outraged husband, fiercely determined to avenge his honor. Maybe he was about to do something tragic. . . . She decided she had to keep him from going to Estello alone. She and Etienne would stay with him. His son's presence would force him to control himself.

Fear abolished her usual reluctance to oppose his decisions. Just as the car was turning into the narrow road that ran through the forest to the farm, she announced in a firm but oddly strained voice that she was not going to wait for him at the farmer's house.

He stopped the car and turned to look at her. The anger on his face had given way to amazement.

"The Nogares are kind, friendly people and I have great respect for them. They'll be delighted to have you as a guest. I'm sure they'll bring out their best wine in your honor."

"I want to go to Estello with Etienne."

"Are you sure you won't change your mind?"

"Yes, I am."

He saw the anxiety in her eyes and smiled faintly, with a touch of irony.

"Will you at least tell me the reason for your sudden aversion to the Nogares?"

Etienne, who had just awakened, spared Pascale the need to lie.

"What did you say, papa? Are we going to see the Nogares? Oh, yes, I can already see the roof of their house! We didn't take long to get here! Come on, let's go! I'll ask César to show Pascale the—"

Rémi interrupted him.

"You have some happy days ahead of you!" he said cheerfully. "But this morning I want you to stay close to the farmhouse. I'll ask Lydia to give you a bath and make lunch for you. Meanwhile Pascale and I will go to Estello to make sure the house is ready, then we'll come back to the farm for you."

He put his hand on Pascale's arm and asked in an undertone, "Are you reassured now?"

Realizing he had guessed her thoughts, she blushed with embarrassment.

"There's César and Lydia!" exclaimed Etienne. "Come on, Parky!"

He jumped out of the car and ran toward a middle-aged couple who had just emerged from a path that intersected the road. The man had a bony face, a handlebar mustache and straightforward good humor lighting up his eyes. The woman, short and thin, with only a few streaks of gray in her black hair, picked up Etienne before coming to greet Rémi.

They gladly consented to take care of Etienne.

"Estello is ready for you, Monsieur Rémi," said Lydia. "The girls cleaned the house and stocked the kitchen. Madame sent them back last night, when she came with your friends, but if you need them again, just say so. I can easily get along without them while you're here."

"Thanks, Lydia," replied Rémi, starting the engine of the car. "I'll come back later and talk it over with you. How's Grandmother Pascaline?"

"She still has her same old aches and pains," said César.

Rémi had to back the car to the road branching off toward Estello. Etienne looked disappointed as he watched his father and Pascale drive away.

"Since you guessed part of the truth," Rémi said bitterly, "why did you want to bring Etienne to Estello? He still doesn't have himself very firmly under control and I don't think he could have handled what he would have discovered there. You were afraid, weren't you? Afraid I might do something violent?"

Choked with emotion and unable to speak, Pascale nodded.

"And now," he went on, "you're thinking, 'He

won't dare to do anything like that in front of me.' You're congratulating yourself on your stratagem. You think your presence will make me hold my anger in check. That's what you think, isn't it? Yes?

"Then let me tell you something you don't know, something I've learned in my career as a lawyer: no one is as deaf and blind as a man determined to get revenge. So if that were what I intended to do, your presence would have no effect on me. Why am I taking you with me? Because our friendship is priceless to me and I feel it would be tarnished if I let you keep the opinion you've formed of me. To make you change that opinion, I'm going to take you into a tragedy. My tragedy. Then maybe you'll understand me better."

He saw Pascale's lips quivering like those of a child on the verge of tears.

"If you'd rather avoid what's sure to be a very unpleasant experience for you," he said more gently, "I'll take you back to the Nogares and you can stay with Etienne. I give you my word that I won't do Andrea any physical harm."

He looked straight ahead and nervously passed his hand over his unshaven cheeks.

Pascale bowed her head, deeply moved by the confidence he was showing in her.

"I'll go with you," she murmured.

The road was bordered by cork oaks and tamarisks. Already heated by the morning sun, the nearby pines gave off a heavy fragrance of resin. The air was filled with the sounds of birds and cicadas. Why did Rémi's morbid jealousy have to poison that joyous vacation atmosphere? How many times had Pascale seen that tormented look on his face when Andrea was late coming home or went off for an appointment with her dressmaker? Why did the same suspicions always come into his mind? And how could he be so sure there wasn't a perfectly innocent reason for what Andrea had done this time? Maybe she had met some friends on the way, invited them to Estello and gone there with them in their car, leaving hers to Irène.

It was a plausible idea, so plausible that Pascale couldn't help suggesting it to Rémi as a possible explanation. He made no comment.

The gate was open. He drove through it without slowing down, then stopped abruptly in the middle of a spacious courtyard paved with large flat stones.

Pascale had expected to find a rustic house similar to the farmhouse she had glimpsed through the pines. But Estello looked more like a monastery than a farmhouse. It had two one-story wings with small windows, joined by an open gallery that faced the courtyard, a kind of cloister with six Romanesque arches. Surrounded by greenery, the two wings and the gallery formed three sides of a square. Rambler roses had climbed up the walls and twined themselves around the columns of the cloister. To the right of the entrance, two palm trees cast their shadows on the red tile roof.

There was no other car parked in the courtyard.

"They've flown the coop, of course," Rémi said sarcastically. "Irène knows how to use a phone."

"Isn't it possible that your friends just brought Andrea here last night and then left?" objected Pascale.

Rémi got out of the car and slammed the door.

"It's time you stopped imagining things," he said brusquely. "Come with me." They walked toward the house together. "And it's also time you realized that Andrea's friends aren't *my* friends." He led her into the living room to the left of the entrance hall. "I don't choose friends who act like barbarians. Just look at that! Look at it!"

Pascale stood in the doorway. In a room where all the furniture seemed to have been carefully chosen to form a harmonious blend of rustic charm and elegant refinement, there was indescribable chaos. Chairs had been overturned. The rug was strewn with broken glasses and bottles. The ashtrays were overflowing and cigarette butts had been crushed on the beautiful inlaid tops of antique tables. A strong smell of alcohol and stale tobacco permeated the air.

Rémi walked across the room and Pascale followed him as if she were in a daze. They went into the dining room. It had evidently been used for dancing, since the rug had been rolled up and the table pushed against one wall, with all the chairs piled on top of it. Rémi bent down, picked up some fragments of china and looked at the plates and dishes that adorned the walls. Several of them were broken.

"Those are rare Samadet china," he said to Pascale. "The last ones were made in 1840. Look at the delicate colors of the birds and flowers painted on them. Since the eighteenth century, generations of Sévriers have lovingly taken care of that collection and handed it down to their children. And in one evening those vandals destroyed a good part of it!"

He put the fragments on the mantelpiece. His hands were trembling.

"This house is what remains of an old Carthusian monastery," he said in a voice made hoarse by anger. "My great-grandfather bought it and renovated it. He also drained and developed thousands of acres of barren moorland that were part of the property. Later, the estate became the family's favorite summer residence. When I was a child I spent all my vacations here. For me, Estello is a peaceful haven full of memories. And you've seen what she's done here. . . . Now do you understand my anger? No, I see only bewilderment in your face. You don't know. You can't know. Come."

He walked through a study and along the cloister. She followed him with the confused unreality of a nightmare. When he came to the end of a long hall in the other wing, he opened the door to a bedroom. Pascale saw open suitcases and a big white bed. In the middle of the bed lay Andrea, asleep.

Rémi went over to her, angrily shook her, took her by the shoulders and made her sit up.

"When you said you wanted to come here, I should have known what your intentions were!" he said. "You had it all worked out in advance. The plan was for you to meet your friends in Bordeaux and come here with them, then Irène would join you a day or so later. But a car accident wasn't part of the program, was it? And you certainly didn't expect to see me here. Don't you ever get tired of lying?"

He shook her again, without getting any response from her. Her eyes stared blankly and there was a lifeless little smile on her lips.

Pascale tried to pull Rémi away.

"Enough! Please stop! Can't you see she's sick?"

He let go of Andrea. She fell back on the bed like a rag doll, muttered a few incomprehensible words, as if she were talking in her sleep, and closed her eyes.

Alarmed by her pallor, Pascale felt her pulse and then lifted her eyelids.

"My God!" she exclained. "Her pupils are dilated as if—"

"As if she were drugged," hissed Rémi. "Good for you, Dr. Nolay! You've made a very accurate diagnosis. But don't worry, your patient will soon come out of her torpor without needing any treatment. I know what I'd find if I wanted to search this room, unless she's found some new drug that she likes even better. With her, anything is possible. There's nothing for us to do but leave her here till the effect wears off. Let's go."

Pascale didn't move. Torn between pity and disgust, she was still looking at Andrea. She wondered if Rémi had tried to cure her and if he still loved her. Then she quickly checked Andrea's pulse again, as if to assure herself that she really was in no danger.

"Come, Pascale."

When she still didn't respond, he put his hand on her shoulder and gently turned her around. She looked at him in silence, with deep distress in her eyes. He led her out of the room. His face was softened by great tenderness.

"I can understand why all this ugliness has upset you," he said. "But there's no need for you to take the tragedy personally. It concerns only me and that creature, and—"

"That 'creature' as you call her so contemptuously, is your wife, Rémi, and also the mother of your son. You have no right to put her out of your heart completely. She's a sick woman, probably so sick that she's not responsible for her acts."

He looked at her with an indefinable expression. Then, after a long silence, he said dully, "Etienne isn't Andrea's son. Or mine either. Irène committed a crime by revealing that secret to him prematurely, but she told the truth. I'll tell you about it later, when you've had some rest, because it's a long story."

Chapter 12

The Estello estate park would have merged into the forest if its boundaries hadn't been marked by hedges. It was an unpretentious park where beeches, oaks and pines grew in graceful disorder. Behind the cloister, two rows of giant laurels interlaced their branches to protect the house from the violent gales that sometimes came from the ocean. But the gentleness of the climate was indicated by the mimosas, dwarf palms and magnolias that bordered the sandy paths.

Pascale was walking rapidly.

"I'll meet you in two hours at the pond," Rémi had said after showing her to her room: a sunny room with flowered cretonne curtains and French doors that opened onto the courtyard. "You won't have any trouble finding it. Just follow the path behind the cloister and you'll come to the pond."

Pascale followed the path into a pine grove, where the way was soon obliterated by a thick carpet of pine needles. She stopped to take her bearings and held up an unopened letter, addressed to her in her mother's handwriting. She had found it in the entrance hall and had taken it with her, intending to read the letter before Rémi arrived.

It was sent directly to Estello and probably arrived the day before. Since she hadn't told anyone but Lambert that she was leaving Versailles, her mother must have learned it from him. But how had she known the address? Pascale had been careful not to give it to Lambert.

After Rémi had left her in her room two hours earlier, Pascale had taken a bath and then tried to rest, but she was so impatient to hear the story he had promised to tell her that she was unable to lie still. She put on sandals and a bright yellow dress and went to the other wing, walking behind the cloister to make sure she wouldn't be seen.

Sensing the humiliation Rémi would feel if he had to tell the servants to clean up the rooms where the orgy had taken place the night before, she set to work. After an hour of hard cleaning, she had succeeded in restoring the living room and dining room to their normal appearance. Then, moved by a concern born of pity, she went to the room where Andrea slept and made sure she showed no alarming symptoms.

She looked around her. To her left, beyond the pines, the pond glittered in the sunlight, clumps of reeds reflected on its surface. It was surrounded by a rim of sandy ground. She took off her sandals and lay down on her stomach with her feet in the water. Then she tore open the envelope and took out the letter from her mother.

DEAR PASCALE,

You may be wondering how I knew where to find you. It wasn't difficult, since the Sévriers' residences are listed in the social register.

I'm surprised to discover that you seem to be holding things back from your family. Why didn't you let me know you were leaving Versailles sooner than you expected? And, more important, why haven't you ever told me about Lambert's feelings for you? If you had, I would have been less disconcerted this afternoon when he came to tell me himself.

Can you imagine Lambert in a dark blue suit, a white shirt and a tie? Well, that's exactly how he was dressed when he came to see me, and it didn't even seem to make him feel uneasy. Maybe he's less of a nonconformist than he'd like people to think. But by the time he'd been talking to me for several minutes he became so irritated by my skepticism that he took off his jacket and tie, unbuttoned his collar and began pacing the floor. Then he told me what was really on his mind. It was so amazing that I sometimes had to interrupt and make him repeat what he was saying, to make sure I hadn't misunderstood.

My common sense told me he was overdramatizing now and then, and I discounted some parts of his story entirely because they conflicted too much with what I know about the Sévrier family. I knew Robert Sévrier, Rémi's father, quite well. He was a rich stockbroker who loved antiques, especially from the seventeenth and eighteenth centuries. A good customer. And a warm-hearted man, too, with great integrity. He was a widower and he lived only for his son, yet toward the end of his life he refused to see him. I never knew what had happened between them. Once he said, "Rémi has chosen a path that leads to ruin and dishonor." But there was such grief in his voice that I couldn't bring myself to question him, and he didn't tell me anything more.

To come back to Lambert, here's the gist of what he told me:

Some time ago he met Andrea Sévrier when she came to his studio to see the works he exhibited at the Festival of Contemporary Sculpture. They took a liking to each other and she introduced him to some friends of hers who found him a job designing a theater set. To thank her, he offered to immortalize her features in stone. (Between you and me, I wonder if she'll recognize herself in the statue!) She wasn't aware that he knew you, or at least that's what he told me. In any case, while she was posing she began confiding in him and told him about the appalling life her husband forces her to lead. According to her, he's a dangerous man with a sick imagination who tries to pervert everyone around him. That seems to be consistent with what his father said about him.

Lambert told me he didn't want to let Andrea know he was engaged to you, though I didn't understand why. But are you really engaged, or is it just something he's imagined? Be that as it may, he's afraid for you. He says he tried to warn you of the danger you're in, but you wouldn't take him seriously.

PASCALE LOOKED UP. A shadow had just fallen across the sheet of paper in her hand.

Rémi was standing in front of her, smiling. She

folded the letter and slipped it into her pocket as she stood up.

"Don't let me interrupt you," he said. "I'll wait while you finish reading your letter."

"No, it doesn't matter, I've already read the most important part. I'll finish it later."

"All right, if you don't mind . . . let's walk along the edge of the pond. A little farther on, there's a bench in the shade. We can sit and talk there."

They began walking side by side, separated by a silence heavy with thought. Rémi held his hands behind his back, clasping and unclasping them as he often did when he was preoccupied.

Pascale glanced anxiously at him now and then. She thought of what she had read in her mother's letter. It was true she had fallen in love with him, but she could see no way in which he had deliberately tried to make it happen. He had simply been himself.

She searched her memory as honestly as she could and concluded that Lambert's suspicions weren't justified by anything Rémi had ever said or done. At least not as far as she was concerned. But she felt a twinge of doubt when she thought of Andrea. The idea that Rémi had never tried to cure her had already crossed Pascale's mind.

Unable to endure her uncertainty any longer, she turned to him and asked more bluntly than she had intended, "Why don't you make Andrea go to a hospital where she can get treatment for her addiction?"

A shadow passed over his face. He went on walking in silence till they came to a shaded stone bench facing the pond.

They sat on it. In front of them, a flat-bottomed boat was rocking gently at the end of the rope that held it near the edge of the water.

"I don't know what's been going on in your mind, but I'm sure you suspect me of being cruel to Andrea," he said bitterly. "You seem to believe I've abandoned her to her addiction without ever having tried to help her overcome it. The truth is that she's already undergone treatment several times, without success. She'd agreed to join me in Switzerland next week, supposedly for a vacation but actually to spend several months in a hospital near Lausanne. I don't know if she still intends to go there, but if she does I'm sure that attempt will be no more successful than the others. She's incurable."

"When did it all begin?"

"In her adolescence, I suppose. She didn't grow up in a very healthy atmosphere. Her father had come to Marseilles after spending years in the Far East, where he was involved in some sort of illegal activity; I don't know exactly what. It seems likely that after he returned to France he carried on the same activity, or something like it, but he died before the police could prove anything against him."

Pascale's look of shocked surprise prompted Rémi to add, "I didn't learn about all that till later, when I'd discovered what Andrea was really like. By then it was too late."

"Too late?"

"I was already married to her. I have no excuse for my blindness. I can't attribute it to the innocence of youth because I was twenty-seven and she certainly wasn't the first woman I'd ever known. I met her on a ship, during a cruise to the West Indies. Irène was with her, and I was touched by their affection for one another.

"When Andrea and I became engaged, I introduced her to my father. He mistrusted her from the start, which shows that his judgment was much better than mine. He began discreetly trying to find out more about her. I didn't know that at the time, but I was irritated by his suspicious attitude. Mainly to spite him, I married her sooner than we'd announced at first.

"Soon after the wedding I discovered her real character. I was horrified to realize I'd married a lying, scheming woman with degrading inclinations that she was completely unable to control. Her conduct before our marriage had been a deliberate effort to keep me from seeing her as she was."

"Why didn't you get a divorce?" asked Pascale.

"Because I'm opposed to it as a matter of principle. Once I've given my word, I don't go back on it. And also, I must admit, in spite of everything I still thought Andrea's case wasn't hopeless. I've long since lost my illusions about that."

"And what was Irène's attitude?"

"She decided to become my ally, in her own interest. With her perfect beauty, Andrea was Irène's revenge against the fate that had made her physically unattractive. She'd always counted on Andrea to make a marriage that would give them both a life of luxury. I was only an undistinguished lawyer at the time, but in the background was my father's huge fortune: farms and woodlands all over France, the Estello estate, houses in Deauville and Versailles. But the income from all that property could be taken away from them by the stroke of a pen. Although I didn't want a divorce, I might ask for a separation. A lawyer is to some extent a public figure. His colleagues, clients and friends are always ready to judge not only his conduct but also his family's. Irène realized that. She's an intelligent woman. I made a kind of unwritten pact with her."

He paused and let his eyes wander over the surface of the pond. Beads of sweat appeared on his forehead. The expression of bitterness aged him. There was no pretense in his attitude. His confession rang so true that Pascale had forgotten her doubts.

"Here's what I demanded," he went on: "Irène would live with us and run the household, since Andrea had no interest in doing so. Andrea could lead the social life she'd always wanted, provided she never let anyone suspect that our marriage was a failure. Irène would see to it that there was never any public scandal.

"Till recently she succeeded quite well, but in the last few months Andrea has been almost impossible for even Irène to control. It's a miracle there hasn't been any gossip yet, at least as far as I know. I had to sell the house in Deauville because I found out Andrea had been meeting her friends there, and you can imagine what went on. This week, Irène couldn't stop her from having another of her gatherings here. Or so she told me. I've learned to mistrust her as much as Andrea."

"And what about Etienne? Where did he come from?"

Rémi's face softened, as it always did when he talked about Etienne.

"Only once, at the beginning of our marriage, I nearly gave in to the temptation of divorce. That was when Andrea told me she could never have any children. She must have realized she'd made a mistake in letting me know, because she immediately said it was one of the greatest sorrows of her life. At that time, I didn't realize how hopeless things were. I still thought Andrea could become a normal woman. I wanted to believe it.

"I was foolish enough to think I could transform her by giving her a chance to develop maternal feelings.

We began looking for a baby to adopt. We visited orphanages for two years. She could never make up her mind; she always found some physical defect in the babies we saw. She was even more cold-hearted than I'd realized: she visited each orphanage as if she were going to a kennel to select a dog she'd be proud to exhibit. I thought she was just covering up her fear of accepting responsibility.

"But finally Etienne caught her fancy. He was two months old, born of unknown parents, and he was by far the most beautiful baby we'd seen. She was amused by him at first, but she soon tired of his demands on her and was surprised by my continuing affection for him. I think she must have imagined that an adopted child could be returned or exchanged, like something bought in a department store. You can imagine how I feel now about the life I have imposed on Etienne because of my blind stupid hope."

"Who took care of him? Irène?"

"Yes, later with the help of a nursemaid. She respected our agreement, but that was all. We had to give others the impression that we were a happy family. Needless to say, her devotion to Etienne was nothing but a pretense. It showed clearly whenever she looked at him. Her expression was a silent reproach to him, the worst kind of all: she reproached him simply for existing.

"While I was completing the adoption procedures, I saw to it that Etienne would have exactly the same rights as if he were really my son. When I told Andrea and Irène about that, I could see they were terribly upset but trying to hide it. They soon began talking about the dangers of heredity. After all, they said, we knew nothing about Etienne's parents, so how could we be sure he wouldn't turn out to have some disastrous hereditary defect? But since we'd known about the risks of adoption before we began looking for a child, their belated misgivings seemed odd to me. I quickly realized they were motivated by self-interest. If I died, Etienne would inherit all my property."

"Oh!"

Pascale hadn't been able to hold back an exclamation of fear. Rémi misinterpreted it as indignant disbelief.

"You don't believe me? Here's proof of what I'm saying: ever since Etienne became my sole heir, Irène has been relentlessly trying to make me put my property in Andrea's name. I've always refused, of course. I have no intention of disinheriting my son in favor of a woman who deserves only contempt."

He fell silent again. There was still sadness in his eyes but he seemed more relaxed, as if his sorrow had been partly relieved by talking about it.

Pascale thought of Etienne and wondered if, in such circumstances, separation might not be better for a child than constant hostility between his parents. With her usual frankness, she told Rémi what was on her mind.

He hesitated before answering.

"Maybe in some cases. But I have no family left, so Etienne would have no loving aunt or grandmother to take care of him. So far I've considered it best to give him at least an illusion of family life. And the fact is that until you came along he seemed to suffer more from lack of motherly love than from the hostility between Andrea and me. I've always done my best not to quarrel with her in front of him."

He smiled. "You've given him what he lacked,

Pascale. I shudder at the thought of how much worse he might have become this summer if it hadn't been for your understanding and love."

"I won't always be with him," she objected gently. "In October I'll go back to medical school."

Rémi's face tensed for a moment, then he shook his head as if he wanted to banish all unpleasant thoughts from his mind.

"That's still a long way off," he said, standing up. "For the next few hours, at least, let's try to forget all the depressing things we've been discussing. Come. We're going to take a short cut through the woods to see the Nogares and bring Etienne back with us."

"But . . . what about Andrea?"

"She won't wake up for a long time yet. The best thing we can do for her is to leave her alone."

Chapter 13

"Parky wants to go for a boat ride on the pond."

Frowning with stubborn concentration, Etienne expressed this demand for the tenth time since the beginning of the meal. Emmanuelle, one of the two Nogares daughters, a tall, dark-haired, cheerful young woman, put a plate down in front of him. He immediately pushed it away. He had been behaving most unpleasantly: being obnoxious, disrupting conversation with deliberately foolish remarks, answering Pascale insolently whenever she gently reprimanded him.

Rémi had scowled at him several times, ready to give him an angry scolding, but he had always been stopped by a pleading look from Pascale. She guessed the reasons behind Etienne's behavior. Rémi was leaving immediately after lunch. Etienne's arrogance was only a defense against his distress.

In the past two days he had been happier than ever before in his life. At Estello, his father had nothing in common with the distant, inaccessible man of Versailles, who nearly always wore a stern look on his face and disappeared just when he was needed most. During those two days, Etienne had been able to approach him at any time, ask him questions that were always answered and bask in the sense of security that came from his calm, reassuring presence.

He looked at Pascale and Rémi with an expression of adoration mingled with rancor.

They were sitting across the table from him in the big dining room, with sunlight on their faces. He noticed that the radiant little flame that had shone in their eyes the past two days had now vanished. Were they sad too? He remembered his own sadness and frowned. Why couldn't those happy days have gone on till the end of vacation? Why was his father leaving so suddenly?

He hadn't believed the reasons the grownups had given him.

"Your mother is sick," Blanche had told him. "She must go to a hospital. Your father will take her there and stay with her till she's well."

Etienne had shrugged. He was sure his mother wasn't sick. But she was mean, no doubt about that! He had seen her walk to where Parky was sleeping peacefully in the courtyard and begin kicking him viciously. "That dirty little mutt doesn't deserve to live!" she had shouted. Then she had shrieked hysterically for a long time.

"She acts like a stepmother," Etienne had thought, remembering Claude's remark: "A stepmother yells all the time and hits you."

After that outburst of uncontrollable rage, Rémi had

called a doctor. Since then, Andrea had stayed in her room, where Emmanuelle brought her meals.

The day before, Etienne had heard her laughing loudly. No, she wasn't sick. So his father was going away just to be rid of him. Luckily he still had Pascale, but for the moment he had a strong urge to exasperate her.

"Parky will go for a boat ride on the pond."

He said it in an imperious tone, looking at them defiantly. Yes, he would get into that tempting boat, in spite of all the times he had been told to stay away from it.

"Parky would wake up the water genie," Pascale explained with apparent calm, although her patience was wearing thin. "He's a powerful genie and doesn't like to be disturbed. I'm afraid it might cost Parky his life."

At last she had deigned to notice that he existed!

"Genies aren't bad," he said belligerently. "The one in Aladdin's lamp did everything Aladdin told him to."

"There are good genies and bad genies," remarked Rémi. "The one in the pond seems to be a bad one, since he doesn't like dogs."

"You hear that, Parky?" said Etienne, bending down. He whispered something under the table, then straightened up with an expression of bravado. "Parky says I can go by myself."

Emmanuelle, who had just brought in a cherry pie, winked at Pascale.

"You mustn't make the genie angry, Etienne," she said in a solemn tone that impressed him against his will. "I saw him once, and it nearly scared me to death! It still scares me when I think of it now! To make it easier for him to catch his victims, he walks on stilts, the way shepherds used to do in this part of the country. His neck is so long he can turn his head in all directions. He wears a red cape and a hat with feathers on it."

"I'm not scared at all!" Etienne said in a faltering voice.

"You're a brave boy," remarked Rémi.

"But I'm sure the genie is smarter and stronger than all the brave boys in the world put together," said Pascale firmly, feeling that Rémi wasn't giving Emmanuelle enough support. "What does he do with his victims?"

"He pulls them down to the bottom of the pond and eats them," answered Emmanuelle.

Etienne's self-confidence was badly shaken. He didn't know what to think. He looked questioningly at each of the three grownups. Pascale and Emmanuelle seemed horrified, but there was a little twinkle in Rémi's eyes. Etienne decided that the genie might not be as ferocious as Emmanuelle had said.

When she had left the dining room, Rémi asked, "Do you still intend to go out in the boat even though you've been told not to?"

Etienne swallowed without answering. His determination was weakening but he didn't want his father to know that. The more he thought about taking that boat ride, the bigger the lump in his throat became. He was afraid he wouldn't be able to hold back his tears.

"Hold out your plate and I'll give you a piece of pie," said Pascale.

"I don't want any pie."

"What are you going to do this afternoon?" asked Rémi, putting his hand on Pascale's arm as a signal for her to remain quiet.

"I'm going out in the boat."

Rémi sighed, then shrugged his shoulders.

"Well, if that's really what you want to do, go ahead. You know the risks, don't you?"

Etienne nodded. The lump in his throat was nearly choking him but he managed not to show his feelings.

"I think I'll have another piece of pie," said Rémi, turning away from him. "I can't imagine how anyone could be foolish enough to pass up such a good dessert!"

He put the piece of pie on his plate with deliberate slowness and began eating with complete absorption.

Etienne was dumbfounded. Was this all the importance his father attached to his refusal to obey? He no longer had any desire to go out in the forbidden boat. And he felt very unhappy.

Pascale stood up.

"We'll have our coffee in the living room," she suggested. "Etienne can take a rest in the courtyard, or maybe he'd rather lie down in the cloister, since it's cooler there."

"I think he'll choose to go to the pond right away and be eaten by the horrible genie," said Rémi. "What a pity!" He added, seeing tears well up in Etienne's eyes. "I was planning to take you and Pascale on a boat ride along the Huchet, a beautiful little stream that passes near here. Since I'll be back in five days—"

"Five days?" Pascale and Etienne exclaimed at once. Both felt a burst of joy. Rémi turned to Pascale with a smile.

"That's right, five days. What's so strange about that? Can't I spend a vacation here if I want to?"

Etienne threw his arms around his father. He no longer tried to hold back his tears, now that they were tears of joy. Parky came out from under the table, barking excitedly.

"Oh, papa, I'm so glad! And that silly Blanche told me you weren't coming back! Pascale is glad too. Look at her—her eyes are shining like stars!"

Pascale blushed and quickly lowered her eyes, embarrassed at being unable to hide her feelings better.

Etienne saw Emmanuelle carrying the coffee tray into the living room and ran off to tell her the amazing news.

"I thought you were going to work on an important case in Geneva," said Pascale, wanting to hear Rémi confirm his decision.

"I'll bring all the papers back with me and work on it here. I made up my mind a little while ago, because I couldn't bear the sadness I saw in Etienne's face. Andrea won't need me in Switzerland, since the hospital doesn't allow any visitors while the treatment is going on. I'll bring Irène with me as soon as I come back. She'll take over the job of running the household, as usual."

Etienne ran into the room and approached Pascale. In a surge of affection that he no longer tried to hold back, he took her hand and kissed it.

"I've changed my mind," he said with a broad smile. "I don't feel like going out in the boat by myself any more."

PASCALE WAS AWAKENED by a ray of sunlight on her face. She automatically raised herself on one elbow to look at her alarm clock and see what time it was. A moment later she remembered that, in her hurried departure from Versailles, she had left her clock behind, along with all her medical books.

"It doesn't matter," she thought. "I still have my wrist watch, and on a day like this I feel more like basking in the sun than studying."

Emmanuelle would bring her breakfast in twenty minutes. Both Emmanuelle and Blanche had developed a sincere affection for Pascale. She stretched with a happy sigh. Here at Estello, she slept peacefully and felt perfectly secure. She remembered the fear that had gripped her during her last night in Versailles. But Estello was even more isolated. Why didn't she feel the slightest trace of apprehension here?

Etienne slept in one of the bedrooms next to hers. The other one was occupied by Emmanuelle and Blanche. At the end of the hall, in a little room that faced the entrance gate, was their uncle Paul, who lived in the nearby village of Castarets and made his living by tapping pine trees for resin. He had agreed to stay in the house at night till Rémi came back.

There were three other bedrooms in that wing. Rémi's was the one closest to the cloister. To keep it from becoming filled with the musty smell that seemed to cling to the old walls, Pascale had opened its windows after he had left. She was surprised to find that his room had a completely different atmosphere from the other bedrooms: no rustic furniture or flowered cretonne, but a canopied mahogany bed, a writing desk and several dressers in the purest Louis-Philippe style. On the wall, beside some Corot reproductions, was a genuine Fantin-Latour portrait of a man in his early thirties. Pascale had noted the resemblance between him and Rémi: the same rather angular features, the same piercing, ironic eyes.

Probably his grandfather, she thought and understood Rémi's attachment to that austere furniture. He undoubtedly regarded it as the relic of a venerated past.

In the three days since his departure she had become better acquainted with all the Nogares. They were simple people, but also generous and proud. They were embittered by Andrea's and Irène's haughtiness toward them. Pascale learned that they had more serious reasons for bitterness, but, too tactful to complain, César and Lydia said nothing about these. Pascaline, the white-haired old grandmother whose alert intelligence still shone in her eyes, said to Pascale, "Monsieur Rémi would be better off living with a tiger than with a wife like his!"

That day, Pascale stayed with her longer than usual. Then, when Etienne went off with César to take care of the animals, Pascaline said what was on her mind.

"Something bad will happen to Monsieur Rémi. You'll see. There's no crime his wife won't commit if she feels like it."

Seeing Pascale's incredulous look, she shook her head sadly and continued: "Blanche and Emmanuelle told me Madame Andrea was going to a hospital for treatment. She ought to stay there and never come out. She's a monster. You know Paul, my second son. He's a big, handsome man. Last year she kept after him for a month. He tried to act like he didn't understand what she wanted. When she finally realized she wasn't going to get anywhere with him, do you know what she did? She poisoned his mule one night, just out of spite."

She paused for a moment, looking at Pascale intently.

"I can tell you I find it hard to believe. . . . When she found out her dog had been killed in a car accident, what did she do? She went after Etienne's dog and nearly kicked the poor little thing to death. That's the way she is: spiteful, vicious, hard-hearted. I know many things, whether you believe me or not. If you keep your eyes open all the time, maybe you can keep something tragic from happening. Watch over Etienne and his father as closely as you can. Reine wrote me that—"

"Reine? The gardener's wife in Versailles?"

"Yes, she's my sister, didn't you know? She wrote me about everything you've done for Etienne. I'm so glad you came along in time! It was the best thing that could have happened to him, but I'm not at all sure Madame Andrea is happy about it.

"Be on your guard against her. Her sister is a dangerous, treacherous woman, but she only does what Madame Andrea wants her to. That one may seem to be unaware of what's going on around her but she has the touch of evil."

As she drank the hot chocolate that Emmanuelle had brought her, Pascale thought of the warning she had been given the day before. It upset her without really alarming her. She felt there was a certain amount of exaggeration in Pascaline's warning, motivated by the whole family's resentment against Andrea.

She was sure Irène was the more dangerous of the two sisters. As for Andrea's intelligence, she considered it insignificant. There was sometimes a strange, disquieting glow in her violet eyes, but Pascale saw it as a sign of incipient derangement. No, she couldn't take Pascaline's apprehensions seriously.

Surely they were the ramblings of a superstitious woman. Recalling the woman's whispered warning of "the touch of evil," she almost smiled. She was willing to keep a close watch over Rémi and Etienne but even if Pascaline was right about Andrea, the fact that she was now in a hospital would lessen the danger.

Pascale was soon to learn how mistaken she was.

Chapter 14

"And now you'll go straight back to Estello without dawdling on the way. Promise?"

"I promise," answered Etienne, and he meant it.

His days with the Nogares were happy ones. After feeding oats to the mule and corn to the chickens, he went with César and Paul to tap some young pines for resin.

Rémi, who had been back at Estello for several weeks, took Irène and Pascale shopping in Bordeaux that day. Etienne was glad to stay behind. Irène's presence took all the fun out of riding in the car, and he would much rather be on the farm with the Nogares than in Bordeaux. So by ten o'clock in the morning he set off for the farm alone, "like a man," as Rémi had said. Pascale was a little uneasy about it, but Rémi, who wanted Etienne to develop a sense of independence, reassured her: "He knows every inch of the road and there are never any cars on it except mine. Nothing can happen to him."

That morning Etienne took the road bordered by tamarisks and cork oaks, then turned where it joined the road to the farm.

He would probably have followed the same route on the way back if a weasel hadn't scurried past in front of him soon after he left the farmhouse. Parky, who was trotting along beside his master with his nose to the ground, saw only a reddish blur that vanished into the underbrush. But the smell aroused his belligerent instincts. He immediately ran after the weasel, ignoring Etienne's efforts to call him back. Nothing mattered to him but following the trail of his enemy. It was an erratic trail that wound through the forest in all directions.

Finally the scent faded away. Parky sniffed energetically but could smell nothing on the ground except the warm fragrance of pine needles. He ran in circles for a few moments, then sat down, disheartened.

He looked around. No sign of his little master. No scent of him in the air, either. A rabbit hopped past a few feet away. Parky made no move to follow it. Completely absorbed in his misery, he began to howl in despair.

When he stopped to catch his breath, he heard a human voice in the distance behind him. He pricked up his ears. It was Etienne's voice! He ran toward the sound, barking joyfully.

"Now we're in a mess!" Etienne said after greeting his dog with more affection than anger. "Because of you, we're lost."

He wasn't particularly worried about it. He had spent so much time in the forest that he regarded it as his friend.

"I'll find the way home, Parky," he said confidently. "Just stay with me."

Except when he turned to avoid clumps of ferns or brambles, he walked in a straight line. This time Parky resisted all tempting smells and stayed close beside his master. The cicadas were giving a deafening concert. Etienne looked for them and was surprised not to see them.

Then all at once, by a stroke of pure luck, he saw the hedge that surrounded the Estello park.

"You see, Parky? I told you I'd find the way," he said, taking this miracle as a matter of course.

He even found a little wooden gate that spared him the unpleasant task of having to push his way through the thorny hedge. On the other side of it, the lane stretched away from him, beneath a vault of foliage. He felt cool air on his face. After the sultry heat of the forest, that breeze gave him new energy. He began running along the lane, with Parky behind him.

The trees soon became farther apart. A dazzling light made Etienne blink his eyes. He stopped. The lane sloped down to the glittering surface of the pond.

He felt a little disoriented because he had never approached the pond from that direction with Pascale or his father. Then he remembered Emmanuelle's story. He picked Parky up and carried him in his arms to protect the dog from the genie of the pond and walked forward very cautiously.

But curiosity soon drove away his anxiety. After all, why not take advantage of this chance to get a look at the genie? Till now he had kept his word. Even though the temptation to go look for the genie had sometimes been very strong, he had never gone to the pond alone. But this time, since he had come there only by accident, his conscience was at ease.

He wouldn't repeat Emmanuelle's mistake by going too close to the water's edge. He was too smart for that! He would stay hidden among the trees and watch the genie without revealing his presence. Then, when he was ready to go to the house, he would walk through the woods, avoiding the path that ran past the pond.

The trouble was he didn't know in which direction the house lay. If only he could see the boat. . . . It was always tied in front of the stone bench, and he knew how to find his way from there.

He went to the place where the path joined the lane and immediately spotted the boat. All around it, the surface of the water was reddened by the glow of the setting sun. He would have to go past it to reach the path to the house.

Still carrying Parky, he began walking silently through the tamarisks. A few moments later his heart leaped into his mouth. Aunt Irène was sitting on the stone bench, reading. He couldn't go much farther without attracting her attention, and he dreaded her more than all the genies in the world. If she saw him there, she would go straight to his father and demand that he be punished for breaking his word.

He decided to wait till she left, but feeling that the tamarisks wouldn't give him enough shelter, he carefully made his way to a clump of tall ferns and peered out from behind it.

It turned out to be the perfect observation post. Not only could he watch everything his aunt did, but by turning his head to the right he could see the reeds of the pond and a good part of its shore.

Sensing that something serious was happening, Parky huddled against him without so much as twitching an ear.

Irène was reading a letter. It must have contained unpleasant news, judging from her angry expression and gestures. At first the sight amused Etienne, but he soon became bored.

He looked toward the reeds rustling in the winds. Suddenly his eyes opened wide and stared at a strange creature near the edge of the pond, apparently observing its surface with great interest.

It was like a big bird, but Etienne had never seen a bird standing on stilts, as this one was doing. Its back and sides were red: its neck was as long and sinuous as a snake; a tuft of feathers rose from its black head; and it had a long, yellow, pointed, threatening beak.

Etienne shuddered and put his arms protectively around Parky. The little dog sniffed the air attentively and caught a whiff of a strange smell he couldn't identify. He bared his fangs and growled.

"Quiet, Parky!" whispered Etienne. "It's the genie! Don't let him know we're here!"

Just then the genie's neck undulated. He disdainfully turned his head away from the pond and eyed the path suspiciously.

Parky took this as a personal insult and growled more loudly. Etienne had difficulty holding him back. He looked anxiously at his aunt, but still absorbed in reading her letter, she was oblivious to everything around her.

The genie pivoted on his stilts and began walking along the shore with majestic slowness, in the direction of the stone bench.

A malicious hope brightened Etienne's face. To make sure he would miss nothing of the scene he was imagining in advance, he crept forward a few inches. A twig snapped under him.

The genie stopped and turned one of his yellow eyes toward the ferns.

Parky couldn't stand it any longer. He slipped away

from Etienne and pushed his way through the ferns, snarling; Etienne managed to catch him by the tail.

The genie saw the little dog and the feathers on his neck bristled with rage. He let out a war cry that made Irène start violently. She leaped to her feet as if propelled by a spring. The genie spread his immense wings, heavily took flight and passed just over her head. She screamed in terror and ran away as fast as her still-bandaged ankle would permit. And in her panic, instead of thrusting her letter into her pocket as she had intended, she dropped it on the ground.

When Etienne recovered from his surprise he clasped Parky in his arms and kissed him.

"You're the bravest dog in the world! You're not afraid of *anything*!"

It was hard for him to grasp what had just happened. A little dog had terrified a powerful, ferocious genie, and Aunt Irène, that formidable dictator who ruled the servants with an iron hand, had ignominiously run away.

WHEN HE ARRIVED at the house he found it in turmoil. Pascale had gone off to look for him. His father, on the verge of panic, was talking of calling the police. Irène was angrily berating Emmanuelle and Blanche for not having found a letter which, she said, had to have been lost somewhere between the pantry and the dining room.

Etienne explained that he had become lost in the forest, but didn't breathe a word about the pond.

In Pascale's absence, Emmanuelle gave him his bath. When he was alone with her, he opened his heart to her. After telling her the whole story of his adventure he added, "And I know where Aunt Irène's letter is: it's on the ground by the stone bench."

Emmanuelle decided she would go and get it the next morning and quietly put it somewhere in the dining room. She knew Irène well enough to be sure she would go on persecuting everyone around her till she got what she wanted.

And when she went to the stone bench for the letter she would go on to the farm and tell César that the big heron that stopped by every year, on its way to Africa, had already come.

But a week later Irène was still looking for her letter and Etienne was laughing up his sleeve at the thought that the genie must have eaten it.

EVER SINCE RÉMI'S RETURN to Estello, something had always come up to prevent him from arranging the holiday boat trip on the Huchet. He felt that a whole day would be needed for it, and he had to spend all his mornings working on the papers he had brought back from Geneva.

To console Etienne, he took him to a beach with Pascale nearly every afternoon. Sometimes they went as far away as Biarritz or Hossegor, but Etienne didn't care where they went as long as Pascale and his father were with him.

His affection for them was shown in thoughtful little gestures that sometimes moved Pascale to tears. If he was gathering shells on the beach, he picked out the prettiest ones for her. Every day he brought a lovingly composed bouquet of wildflowers from the park or the woods and gave it either to her or to Rémi, depending on which of them had received a bouquet the day before.

"He mustn't become too dependent on me," she kept telling herself, thinking of their inevitable separation.

She wondered if Rémi was displeased to see Etienne becoming so strongly attached to someone who was only passing through his life. What other explanation could there be for the expression of pain or dissatisfaction that all too often darkened his face? In the past, she would have assumed he was thinking of Andrea, but she now knew his true feelings for his wife.

Furthermore he had said he regarded Andrea's stay in the hospital as a wonderful respite. But the future was still dark for him, and Pascale's spectacular success with Etienne hadn't solved the long-range problem of how the child was to be brought up. Considering his attachment to her, she sometimes wondered anxiously if her efforts might eventually turn out to have done more harm than good.

So for some time now she had been trying to stay in the background as much as possible. And, painful though those sacrifices were to her, she refused to go with Rémi and Etienne on their excursions. Perhaps she was also trying to test herself by partially giving up her greatest source of happiness: being with Rémi.

They went without her to Arcachon, the oil wells at Parentis and the seaplane base at Biscarosse. But they both came back from those outings with glum faces and a tendency to lapse into ill-humor.

As they were eating dinner on the evening after the visit to Biscarosse, Rémi announced that they could finally take their boat trip on the Huchet the next day, if the weather was good. He looked intently at Pascale as she sat across the table from him, but she deliberately wore an expression of indifference.

"You'll come with us this time, won't you, Pascale?" he asked in a voice vibrant with hope.

"Say yes, Pascale," Etienne insisted without giving her time to answer. "It's so much more fun when you're with us!"

"I think the seaplanes would have been more interesting this afternoon if you'd been there to watch them with us," added Rémi. "But I don't know why we're talking like this," he added brusquely, "since that boat trip has been planned and accepted since the beginning of our vacation."

Irène's shifty little eyes had been moving from one face to another.

"You're talking mainly to yourself, Rémi," she said caustically. "Pascale hasn't refused. She'll be only too glad to come with us."

"Why *too* glad?" Pascale replied with a hostility that surprised even her.

Irène gave her a venomous look, quickly followed by a bland smile.

"Please don't misinterpret what I said. I was thinking only of your maternal feelings. They're so obvious that—"

"That's enough, Irène."

Rémi had stood up with anger blazing in his eyes. Etienne unintentionally warded off the storm that was about to burst. He was alarmed by something Irène had said.

"Is Aunt Irène coming with us?" he asked.

"Of course," she said in a reassuring tone, pretending to believe he was worried that he might not have the pleasure of her company. "It's a family outing, isn't it?"

Etienne was about to make an insolent reply when Rémi stopped him with a gesture and said decisively, "The boat I'm going to rent will hold only three people. And you wouldn't enjoy that kind of excursion anyway, Irène. Tell Blanche to pack a picnic lunch for us. We'll leave at about nine o'clock."

A LITTLE LATER, after putting Etienne to bed, Pascale went out into the park. She looked up at the cloudless sky. "I'm sure the weather will be good tomorrow," she thought happily.

The breeze brought her the heady fragrance of a clump of reseda. Her walk along the path held no other goal than breathing the invigorating evening air and putting her thoughts in order.

She was filled with eager anticipation at the idea of spending a whole day with Rémi. She had been resolutely trying to hide her love. That was all she could do. By the time she had become aware of it, it was already so firmly rooted in her heart that she didn't have the strength to tear it out.

She walked slowly in the last lingering glow of twilight, berating herself for not realizing what was happening before it was too late. Suddenly she was startled by the sight of someone coming toward her. When she recognized Rémi, she had a moment of panic and quickly turned back. He hurried forward and stopped her.

"I was looking for you, Pascale," he said in his deep voice. "I want to talk to you."

She looked up at him but the cedars that lined that part of the path enveloped him in shadow and she couldn't see his expression.

They began walking side by side.

"For several days now, you've been avoiding me," he said. "Why?"

"I'm not avoiding you," she answered dully.

Her heart was pounding wildly. She tried to calm herself, without success.

"It's too bad I can't see your eyes. They, at least, never lie."

She stiffened. He took her arm and squeezed it affectionately, as though to ask her to forget what he had just said.

"I think I can guess your reasons," he went on. "I admire their nobility, but I don't agree with them. Etienne needs you. Don't forget that he's barely recovered from the anxiety aroused in him by Irène's malicious remark. He knows he's loved now, but he still needs proof of it. You don't have the right to deprive him of that proof."

She regained some of her self-assurance, now that her thoughts had turned from Rémi to Etienne.

"Don't you realize that I'm with him only temporarily? In a month, he'll have to forget me. If he's too strongly attached to me, the separation may be so painful that it will destroy everything I've been able to accomplish with him. I'd give anything to be sure he won't suffer!"

They walked for a few moments in silence. The air was heavy with the warm smell of the nearby pine forest.

"Pascale," he asked softly, "did you decide to become a doctor out of a really strong sense of vocation?"

"No. My inclination was to work in a nursery school, but my mother insisted that I go to medical school and I finally gave in to her."

"Would it be a very big sacrifice for you to interrupt your medical studies?"

She didn't answer. He was still holding her arm and

she felt his hand tremble. She sensed what he was about to ask. She was suddenly afraid of her own weakness.

"Your silence tells me you've understood," he said dejectedly, "and I'm sure you consider me arrogant for even thinking of asking such a sacrifice of you. For a long time now, I've been hoping you might stay on indefinitely to take care of Etienne, but I've always known it was really too much to expect. I wouldn't have dared even to mention it to you if I hadn't known how much you care about him. With you, he's learned to smile again. And so have I . . . I wanted to keep you. . . . It was only a foolish dream and I'll never say anything more about it. But before I drop the subject forever, I want you to know that I intended to lessen your sacrifice as much as I could by making a financial arrangement that would have enabled you to—"

"Staying with Etienne wouldn't have been a sacrifice," she interrupted.

"Then why don't you want to do it?"

He stopped at the edge of a lawn. The darkness wasn't complete here, since there were no trees to cast their shadows. He made her turn to face him and tried to see what was in her eyes.

If he hadn't been holding her firmly by both elbows, she would have run away to escape the sound of his voice. The emotion she heard in it seemed a trap that was ready to close on her. She had never loved him as much as she did at that moment. She had thought her love was a noble sentiment beyond the realm of physical attraction, but she was discovering that it could become a consuming flame that threatened to destroy all her strength.

Staying with Etienne would have been the easy course to follow, since it would have meant staying with Rémi too. But she had to resist that temptation.

"I can't do it," she said. "It's impossible . . . for personal reasons."

"Family reasons?"

"Yes, maybe. . . . Oh, please don't make me talk about it anymore!"

There was so much pain in her voice that he stopped questioning her. He looked at her in perplexity for a few seconds, then they began walking again.

"Please forgive me," he said after a silence. "I must seem disgustingly selfish to you. My only excuse is that I'm weary and completely disheartened. After years of unhappiness I finally managed to achieve a certain calm by accepting my misfortune. But now I'm forced to admit to myself that I've failed in what I was trying to do for Etienne. I've given him only a caricature of family life and I've come to realize how harmful it would be for him to go on living in such an atmosphere of indifference and animosity. So I've made a decision. I've already told Andrea about it. I'm going to take action for a legal separation. I'll give Andrea and Irène a decent income but they won't live with me.

"But even though I'm sure Etienne will be better off with the separation than without it, I'm still worried about the kind of life he'll lead after it happens, and that's one reason why I was hoping you'd stay with us longer. Only your love could protect him and give him what he needs. In spite of all my efforts to prevent it, he's already been deeply wounded once. Who knows what may happen to him in the future?"

Pascale didn't answer immediately. Her throat was so tight she couldn't speak.

They walked behind the cloister, went around the wing containing the bedrooms and crossed the courtyard. The wrought-iron lanterns on the corners of the house gave off a golden light that made the park seem darker.

As they were about to leave each other she looked up into his eyes.

"I'll stay with Etienne," she said quietly.

Chapter 15

Blanche had prepared the picnic lunch and packed it in three bags. Etienne carried them to the car. He was bubbling over with enthusiasm. Although he usually slept late, this morning he had risen at dawn and Pascale had had a hard time keeping him from pounding on all the bedroom doors to wake up everyone else.

Rémi was smiling and relaxed. He seemed younger and his dark eyes sparkled joyously.

Everyone in the house was cheerful except Irène. She was in a particularly foul humor. She claimed to have found evidence that someone had opened one of the drawers of her writing desk and looked through its contents. She was sure it had been done by either Blanche or Emmanuelle. She didn't dare to include Pascale in her accusations, but the murderous looks she gave her left no doubt about her thoughts.

Irène's usual mistrust had become a real mania. If

she was called to the telephone in the entrance hall, she locked the doors so no one could hear what she was saying. Every morning she hurried out to meet the mailman so that she would be the first to look through the day's letters, and then she locked herself in her room to read hers.

One day when Pascale had asked for news of Andrea, Irène looked at her suspiciously, then said with clear hatred, "What makes you think Andrea has been writing to me?" She walked away without another word.

But that morning, in spite of her vitriolic accusations, she didn't succeed in making Pascale, Rémi and Etienne lose any of their lightheartedness before they left for their outing.

THE SUN WAS ALREADY HIGH in the sky when Rémi stopped the car at the edge of Léon Pond, where their boat ride was to begin. A light mist added a pearly sheen to the surface of the water. Rémi went over to a spot where several boats were tied along the shore and, after talking awhile with the owner, rented one of them.

"Why was that man frowning?" Pascale asked later. "He almost acted as if he didn't want to rent us the boat."

"He didn't think we should go all the way to the ocean," answered Rémi, rowing vigorously. "He said the wind had shifted to the west and might bring a storm."

Etienne examined the blue sky without seeing anything that looked alarming to him. Pascale shared his optimism.

Rémi continued rowing. His arm muscles rippled

under his tanned skin. His whole body gave an impression of peaceful strength. The thought of how good it would feel to rest her head on his shoulder flashed through Pascale and made her gasp. She turned her head away to hide her agitation.

Rémi skillfully avoided clumps of reeds and the treacherous stems of water lilies.

"I've rowed up and down this stream so many times in my childhood that I could do it with my eyes closed," he said.

"Then close your eyes, papa," Etienne challenged him.

Rémi answered by splashing water on him with one of the oars. Some of it also fell on Parky, who was sitting in the bow of the boat. He shook himself energetically. Drops of cold water trickled down Rémi's neck and he protested loudly.

"I'm hungry," said Etienne. "Can I open one of the bags?"

"Wait till we stop," said Pascale. "It won't be long."

Rémi stopped rowing and pointed to a sandbar ahead. In the middle stood a long-legged bird with black and white feathers and a slender beak that curved upward.

"Look, an avocet. They usually stay on the coast. Seeing this one so far inland makes me think the boatman may have been right when he said a storm was coming. . . . I never saw such a big one before. They're usually the size of pigeons."

"What did you call him, papa?"

"An avocet."

Etienne shook his head and looked at Rémi with amused condescension.

"That's not what he is, papa. He's a genie, only he's

not as pretty as the one in our pond. I saw him."

"In that case, you'd better hold onto Parky," said Pascale.

Etienne smiled indulgently. He felt so much more experienced than the two grownups!

"Parky isn't afraid of genies."

Rémi rowed the boat into a narrow stream that branched off from the Huchet. They were soon moving under a vault of foliage so dense that they felt as if they were in a tunnel. The heat turned sultry and the vegetation became denser and almost tropical. In some places the green canopy overhead was so low they had to bend down to pass under it.

Kneeling in the bow, Etienne gave himself the illusion of guiding his father.

Pascale was living a dream. The three of them were a tenderly united family. The charm of that mysterious stream increased the feeling of unreality that nurtured her fantasy.

"Look out, papa! A snake!"

It was only a twisted root emerging from the water.

"We're hunters in the jungle!" Etienne announced triumphantly.

He let out a loud whoop to frighten away any alligators that might be lurking along the bank.

"Let's stop here and have lunch," said Rémi.

When they had climbed from the boat, the mundane task of unpacking the food brought Pascale out of her dream. She wasn't a wife and mother, she was only a friend. It took her a few minutes to shake off her sadness at having to leave the blissful realm her imagination had taken her to.

They sat in a beautiful little clearing at the water's edge. The enchanted silence was broken only by the murmur of the stream and the chirping of birds.

It seemed that nothing could change Rémi's carefree good humor. Even when he discovered that the bottle of wine he had put in the water to cool had been swept away by the current, he laughed as much as Etienne. Yet it seemed to Pascale that he never lost a chance to observe her. Several times she looked up and saw his eyes fixed on her with thoughtful attention.

By the time they had finished their meal, clouds were scudding across the sky. But since there were still large patches of blue, Rémi decided to go on to the ocean.

When they emerged from the forest, the bright sunlight made them shade their eyes with their hands. Rémi continued rowing till they reached a bend in the stream. Soon they could hear the ocean roaring behind a line of sand dunes and the wind left a taste of salt on their lips.

"Can we go swimming, papa?"

A flock of seabirds passed overhead. Rémi anxiously examined the dark clouds that now blotted out the horizon.

"I don't think we'll have to go swimming to get wet," he said.

Just then, as though to justify his worry, a gust of wind blew stinging sand against their faces and drove the boat into a clump of reeds.

"We'd better turn around and go back," said Pascale.

Rémi agreed. He began rowing upstream with the wind at his back. Birds wheeled in the leaden sky, harbingers of the storm. The bright sunshine had given way to a gloomy half-light.

Etienne had lost his gaiety. He sat with Parky on his lap, listening to the trees along the banks of the stream moaning in the wind. Each frown he saw on Rémi's face increased his anxiety.

Pascale, who had a deep dread of storms, forgot her own fear to reassure Etienne. She knew it would do no good to reason with him, so she decided to distract him. She began singing an old song she had learned as a child from her grandmother. Rémi looked at her in surprise at first, then he understood. After giving her a grateful smile he began singing along with her, and soon Etienne joined in too.

The three of them were still singing when they reached Léon Pond. They had been in a driving rain for more than an hour. The boatman offered to let them come into his house and dry their clothes but they went straight to the car and wrapped themselves in the blankets that covered the seats.

THE DRIVE LEADING TO ESTELLO was strewn with broken branches and the rain had left deep furrows in it.

As they were approaching the gate, they saw Irène coming toward them, wearing a black raincoat.

"You have to take me to Castarets immediately," she said to Rémi when they had stopped. "The electricity is off because of the storm and I don't have a single candle in the house."

"Wouldn't it be simpler to send Emmanuelle to the farm for some lanterns?" objected Rémi.

But she insisted on going to Castarets. She was determined to have her candles.

"Furthermore," she said, "we're out of bread. It will take only a few minutes to get to the village. But you'll have to go to the highway on this road, because the short cut is blocked by a tree that was blown down during the storm."

Two roads went from Estello to the highway. The

one that Rémi had to take would force him to make a dangerous turn: he would have to approach the highway at a place where visibility was very limited, cut across the traffic coming from his left, turn and merge into the traffic going in the other direction, toward Castarets.

He grudgingly agreed to do it.

"I'll take Pascale and Etienne to the house, then we'll go to the village."

"There's no need to waste time on that," said Pascale, opening the door of the car. "Come on, Etienne, bring Parky and we'll run to the house."

"Get in, Irène," said Rémi. "But when we come to the crossing, you'll get out and let me know when the highway is clear."

"That's exactly what I intended to do," she retorted.

Something in her voice made Pascale suspicious. She suddenly remembered old Pascaline's apprehensions. She watched Irène get into the front seat beside Rémi. Under the black hood of the raincoat, her face seemed even more secretive than usual. With her thin lips and cold little eyes, she had a look of cruel craftiness that sent a chill up Pascale's spine.

The door closed. Rémi turned the car around and headed back toward the highway.

Pascale shuddered. She was certain that Rémi's life was threatened.

"Hurry to the house with Parky," she said to Etienne. "I'm going to try to catch up with your father because there's something I want him to get in the village and I forgot to tell him about it."

Etienne obeyed. Pascale ran through the woods to cut across the curve that the sideroad made before joining the highway. Hampered by ruts and fallen branches, the Rolls-Royce had gone so slowly that she reached the point where the sideroad joined the highway just as Irène was walking across the highway to stand and watch for traffic.

A dense, fine rain was falling. Looking through the semicircle swept out by the windshield wiper, Rémi was watching Irène and waiting for her signal to start forward. Close behind him, but out of his angle of vision, Pascale had climbed the embankment and was looking at the curve in the main road. It was a sharply banked curve, so that cars approached it without slowing down.

Irène waited while a bus roared past. It was closely followed by a Peugeot. Then, a little farther back, but not at all far enough to give Rémi time to complete his turn, a big truck started around the curve.

The Peugeot passed the sideroad. Just then, even though her view of the highway was even better than Pascale's, Irène signalled Rémi that the way was clear.

At the speed he was going, the driver of the heavy truck couldn't possibly swerve or stop in time to avoid crashing into the Rolls-Royce if it came out in front of him.

In one horrible instant, Pascale realized Irène's intention. She dashed out in front of Rémi's car, ignoring the danger to herself. He had just started up toward the highway when he saw her out of the corner of his eye. He slammed on the brakes but a moment later there was in impact that he felt in every fiber of his body. As he threw open the door, the huge mass of the truck hurtled past him and on down the highway.

Pascale was lying unconscious in front of Rémi's car, with mud and blood on her face. Rémi cautiously picked her up.

Irène ran toward him, seemingly horrified.

"I signalled you not to start!" she said. "Why—"

"Don't bother putting on an act," he said with restrained fury. "I know exactly what you tried to do. Help me put Pascale on the back seat. I want to examine her out of the rain."

The bumper had struck Pascale on the legs and she had also received a hard blow on her head and one shoulder, probably when she fell. A cut in her forehead was bleeding heavily. But she seemed to have no broken bones.

"Get into the car," he ordered Irène. "I'll take Pascale to the house and call the doctor. If he thinks she needs to be in a hospital, I'll drive her to Bordeaux. As for you, I want you to pack up immediately. I think you know why."

"You're dismissing me as if I were a servant," she said bitterly. "But where do you want me to go?"

He felt like answering, "To hell," but he controlled himself.

"You can stay in Versailles till the legal separation goes into effect. After that, I'll see. . . . Tomorrow morning a taxi will come to take you to the station."

By the time they reached the house, Pascale had regained consciousness. Rémi helped her out of the car and then, seeing how weak she was, he carried her into the living room, where a fire was burning in the fireplace. He stretched her out on the sofa and went to call the doctor while Blanche and Emmanuelle took care of her.

When the doctor had carefully examined her, he announced that she had no serious injuries. He gave her a sedative, told her to rest completely and promised to come back the next day.

Wearing her pajamas and a wool bed jacket borrowed from Lydia, she dozed on the sofa for a long time. Since the living room was easier to heat than the bedrooms, it was decided that she would stay there till she recovered.

Before going to bed, Etienne came to kiss her good night. He was awed by her pallor and the bandage on her forehead. He tiptoed out of the room, deeply distressed. He had never said his prayers as fervently as he did that night.

TOWARD MIDNIGHT PASCALE BEGAN to emerge from her torpor. She made a movement. Sharp pain shot through her shoulder and woke her up completely. She opened her eyes and saw that she was lying in the living room. The mist that had enveloped her mind was dispersed. Her first clear memory was of Irène signalling Rémi to go to his death. The truck . . . a red truck that she could have described in sharp detail. . . .

She closed her eyes, chilled with horror. Rémi! What had become of him? She anxiously murmured his name.

"I'm here, Pascale. Please be calm."

His warm, tender voice soothed her. She kept her eyes closed to savor the happiness his presence gave her. Before she looked at him, she had to make sure her face wouldn't betray her emotions.

"Pascale. . . ."

His tone was so vibrant that she opened her eyes. He was there, leaning over her, attentive and concerned.

"Pascale," he went on, "why did you risk your life to save mine? Why? I have a right to know."

She hadn't expected that question. It went straight to the depths of her soul. She tried to turn her head away but he gently prevented her. She felt the pressure of his hand on her cheek as if it were a burn.

"Tell me, Pascale."

He looked into her eyes and knew the truth. His face turned pale and he slowly straightened up.

"Was it for the same reason that you first refused to stay with Etienne after the end of summer?"

She nodded faintly, speechless with shame. She wished the earth would open and swallow her up.

He pulled an armchair close to the sofa and sat on it without once taking his eyes off her blushing face. She no longer tried to avoid his gaze. With her will vanquished and her thoughts in wild disarray, she silently confessed to him what she had tried so hard to keep secret.

"I told you yesterday that you'd taught me to smile again," he said softly. "That was only a half-truth. Your presence has done much more than brighten my life: it's showed me what real love is. Because I love you too, Pascale. I should have tried to put you out of my mind from the start, but I didn't have the strength. I let my love for you continue to grow because it gave me back my will to live."

Pascale felt lightheaded and everything around her seemed blurred, almost immaterial. Rémi's confession had filled her with a joy that swept away the bitter realities of their situation, at least for the moment.

"I can't tell you how happy you've made me by letting me know you share my love," he went on after a silence. "But we're both too overwhelmed with emotion to make any kind of valid decision now. We have to give ourselves time to think calmly and clearly. And to do that, I'm afraid we'll have to accept the painful sacrifice of being away from each other. I'll tell Etienne I have to leave because of my work, but that I'll call him every day. Come to think of it, I wonder if. . . ."

He frowned, thought for a few seconds, then said,

"Yes, I think it would be best for him to stay with the Nogares for a while. He's very fond of them and he'll be delighted to lead the life of a farm boy. I'll tell him you have to go and rest in the mountains to recover from your accident."

"But I don't intend to leave him," she interrupted, looking at him in surprise.

He took on a worried expression.

"You wouldn't be safe here or in Versailles. I'd be afraid of what Andrea or Irène might do to take revenge."

"They might also try to do something to Etienne."

"No. He wouldn't be in danger unless he'd inherited my property."

"I don't understand."

"If I died, Etienne would inherit my whole fortune. And if he died after I did, Andrea would inherit everything. I'm now convinced that she and Irène planned to kill me first, and then Etienne. The first part of the plan nearly succeeded today.

"I have proof that what Irène did was premeditated. The electricity in the house was cut off by taking out the fuses, and there's no fallen tree on the road to the highway. She lost and she knows it. But I don't like the way she looked at you. Don't you see? You may be in some danger."

He took Pascale's hands in his, then kissed them gently, almost religiously.

"I love you, Pascale. The thought of you will help me to go on living."

She later remembered with heartrending sadness the look on his face at that moment, a look of infinite tenderness that stirred her even more than the only physical act by which he had ever allowed himself to express his love.

As Remi walked slowly from the room and through the darkened doorway, Pascale shivered; the premonition she had sensed momentarily sent a ghostly chill through her heart.

Chapter 16

"Since you'll be going through Paris," said Lydia, "I wish you'd call Reine from there and ask her to send me Etienne's winter clothes. The weather will soon be turning cold."

With the help of the Nogares family, Pascale was putting her suitcases into the taxi for her ride to the train station at Dax. After staying with Etienne till October, she was at last obeying Rémi's repeated orders.

He had called Estello every morning at the same time. Etienne had always answered the telephone and talked with him a while, then handed the receiver to Pascale. And from Brussels, Aix, Paris or Geneva, Rémi always urged her to leave Estello.

She kept delaying her departure. She was reluctant to leave Etienne, and she refused to believe she was in any serious danger. She was much more worried about Rémi's safety than her own. But finally, since

Etienne seemed perfectly willing to stay with the Nogares, she told Rémi she would return to Paris and resume her medical studies.

"No, you mustn't do that," he had said. "Irène knows your address. I don't want you to take any risks, even if they seem insignificant to you."

"I'm not the one who's in danger, Rémi, it's you."

"If Irène and Andrea have decided to do anything against me, I'm sure they'll try to do it through you, though I can't say how. But I have a feeling this is the lull before the storm. Andrea has written me from Switzerland that she accepts my decision to apply for a legal separation and won't oppose it in any way. I don't like to see difficulties vanish so easily. It's not normal. There's some kind of treachery hidden behind her sudden meekness. . . . And I'm terribly afraid for you."

Pascale then decided to stay with her grandparents in Burgundy, after a brief visit to her mother in Paris, and Rémi approved of that idea. She hoped she would later be able to have Etienne come and join her.

On the train to Paris, she felt a pang in her heart as she remembered her last image of Etienne: standing in the middle of the courtyard, trying to hold back his tears. He was unhappy, but because he had lost the feeling of rejection that had embittered him in the past, his sorrow was free of rancor. The certainty of being loved had made him a child like any other, a child who would play happily with his schoolmates and forget the sadness of separation.

BECAUSE SHE DIDN'T WANT to alarm her mother, Pascale hadn't told her about Rémi's fears or described the real circumstances of her accident.

She realized her mistake the day after her arrival,

when her mother informed her that since Irène had called to ask about her the week before, she had given her the exact date Pascale would come to Paris.

"Did you also tell her I was going to Burgundy?"

"No. She just wanted to know if you were here or at Estello, so she could send you some things you'd forgotten to take with you when you left Versailles. Some medical books and an alarm clock, I think she said. I told her you'd come and get them yourself, some time this week. And speaking of medical books, I just can't understand why you've decided not to go back to school."

Pascale was no longer listening. If Irène knew of her arrival in Paris, Pascale wondered whether events would justify Rémi's apprehension. She was more curious than worried. She had never seriously believed she was in any danger from Irène. She regarded Irène as an ambitious woman capable of selling her soul to the devil if he offered the right price, but she couldn't imagine her committing a purely gratuitous act of vengeance.

She decided that since she was already expected in Versailles, she would go there and choose Etienne's winter clothes herself.

TWO DAYS LATER SHE WENT to the house in Versailles. Reine opened the gate for her.

"Ah, it's you, Pascale. I'm so glad to see you! We have a terrible problem, but maybe you can help us with it. How's Etienne?"

As she talked, she led Pascale toward the little cottage she shared with her husband, Gaston, the gardener. He was raking dead leaves under the elms. When he saw Pascale he hurried to her as fast as his rheumatism would permit.

She was amazed to learn that Andrea had arrived four days earlier; and every night since then she had been holding parties that "Monsieur Rémi wouldn't like at all."

"When he stopped by here a month ago," said Gaston, "he told us to let him know if anything abnormal happened, but now we can't get in touch with him. We tried to call him in Brussels but he wasn't there. He's not in Geneva, either. At his office in Paris they told us no one is allowed to give out his address. They said we could leave a message and he'd get it very soon, but what we have to tell him is so personal that he wouldn't want anyone else to hear it. You know how he's always been worried about scandal."

"Why don't you send him a letter addressed to his office?" suggested Pascale. "I'm sure they'll forward it to him."

"That's a good idea," said Reine. "I never thought of it. How stupid of me. I'll write to him immediately. You wouldn't believe the things that have been going on here!"

Pascale also learned that Clotilde and Berthe had left, not wanting to go on working for Irène, and that a new maid had been hired. The cook, however, was still there. Serge, the chauffeur, was traveling with Rémi.

She had no desire to see Andrea. Not that she felt there would be anything improper about her visiting Rémi's wife; her conscience was clear on that score. But that soulless, unscrupulous woman aroused deep repugnance in her.

When the new maid let her into the entrance hall, she asked to see Irène.

"She's not here now," replied the maid, "but I can take you to Madame."

Pascale couldn't refuse. Since the maid didn't know her, she wouldn't allow her to go straight up to Etienne's room and take his clothes.

Andrea received her in a boudoir next to the main drawing room, where she was writing a letter. Pascale was struck by the change in her face. Despite skillful makeup, there were dark circles around her violet eyes. Her hollow cheeks and the sagging of her facial muscles showed that her health had deteriorated. Her left hand, resting on the writing desk in front of her, had a slight tremor. Although the room was quite warm, she wore a thick quilted satin dressing gown.

When Pascale came in, she stood up and showed great surprise. A pleasant surprise, judging from the way her eyes glowed.

After sending the maid away, she insisted that Pascale sit down and talk with her till teatime. Pascale curtly declined the invitation and said why she had come.

Andrea didn't seem at all put out by her coldness.

"I'll ring for Suzanne," she said, smiling graciously. "She'll pack up Etienne's clothes and meanwhile we can talk."

"No, don't disturb her," protested Pascale. "I want to pick out the clothes he'll need."

"As you like," Andrea said with a little gesture of discouragement, "but I'd have enjoyed having you stay with me a while." She turned her head away and looked sadly at the leafless trees in the park. Then she asked abruptly, "Do you know anyone who has a toy poodle for sale?"

"A toy poodle?"

"Yes. I've been told they make very affectionate pets, and I'm so lonely. . . . Do you happen to know anyone who has one for sale?"

Pascale shook her head. *Even her voice has changed,* she thought. *It's rough and hoarse now.*

"Then I'll go back to my drudgery," Andrea said wearily. "I've been writing letters to a long list of kennels, to ask if they have any toy poodles. But look how my hand is shaking. I'm so tired my writing is becoming illegible. I still have six more letters to write and I don't think I'll be able to do them all. If only I knew how to type! I could use the typewriter in Rémi's study and finish off my letters in a few minutes."

Pascale's dislike of Andrea was overcome by a vague feeling of pity.

"Would you like me to type them for you?" she asked.

"Oh, yes! Thank you!" Andrea exclaimed joyfully. "Here's the list of kennels and a copy of the letter. I'm so tired I'm going to lie down a while. I'll see you again before you leave, won't I?"

She rang for the maid.

"Take Mademoiselle Nolay up to the second floor. She'll probably need your help. Don't disturb me for any reason. I'm going to my room to rest."

Pascale sent the maid to the attic to find a suitcase, then she went to Etienne's room and began sorting out his clothes. When the maid came in with the suitcase, Pascale thanked her and told her she could leave.

Etienne's winter clothes showed that they hadn't been put away with care. Some of the wool garments had moth holes in them and Pascale had to spend a good part of the afternoon repairing the damage as best she could. Then she typed Andrea's letters.

As she was coming out of Rémi's study she encountered the maid, who looked at her suspiciously. Or at least that was Pascale's impression, though she didn't give it any thought.

She had put the six typed letters on the writing desk in the boudoir and was on her way back to Etienne's room to pick up the suitcase she had left there when she saw Irène running wildly down the stairs.

"Oh, Pascale! I'm so glad you're still here! Come quickly!" She led Pascale into Rémi's study, closed the door and showed her an empty bottle that had contained sleeping pills. "Andrea has tried to kill herself!"

Pascale stifled a cry of alarm. She was trembling in every limb but she at least had the presence of mind to pick up the telephone.

"I'll call Dr. Bernier," she said, remembering the name of the doctor Rémi had wanted to call when Etienne had been half-drowned in the basin.

Irène seized her by the wrist and made her put down the receiver.

"No! Bernier mustn't know about this. No one must know. It's not her first attempt. We'll save her ourselves. You've studied medicine; you know what to do for this kind of poisoning, don't you?"

Pascale made a strenuous effort to remember what she had learned on the subject, without success. She felt as if her brain were paralyzed.

"For a fourth-year medical student, you don't know much," Irène said scornfully. "You have to inject a strychnine solution. Rémi used to keep a prescription for it here. He was always afraid Andrea might try again. I hope the prescription is still here—" She rummaged in a drawer. "Yes, here it is. Take it to the pharmacist. Hurry, there's no time to lose!"

Pascale glanced at the sheet of paper that Irène

handed her. It bore the name and address of the doctor who had taken care of her at Estello.

Seeing her surprise, Irène explained rapidly, "Last fall, Andrea tried the same thing at Estello. As a precaution, the doctor wrote two prescriptions."

"But this one isn't valid," objected Pascale. "There's no date on it."

Irène shrugged her shoulders.

"Of course not! How could anyone know when she might make another attempt? What matters is that the prescription is signed." She took a pen from the desk and held it out to Pascale. "Here, put today's date on it. I'm too upset to hold a pen steady enough to write anything."

A memory flashed into Pascale's mind and swept away her hesitation: she recalled being in a hospital with a group of other medical students when the head physician pointed out a patient suffering from barbiturate poisoning and mentioned treatment with strychnine as one possibility. She dated the prescription and hurried off to the nearby pharmacy.

A quarter of an hour later she brought the strychnine into Andrea's room.

Andrea lay on her bed with her eyes closed. Her face was gray and she was breathing with difficulty. Irène was taking her pulse.

"Hurry, she's sinking fast. I've already sterilized the hypodermic."

Pascale gave the injection. As she was withdrawing the needle, there was a knock on the door. Irene opened it.

"You rang, Mademoiselle?" asked the maid, taking in the scene at a glance: Andrea on the bed, Pascale with the hypodermic in her hand.

"Yes," said Irène. "Call Mademoiselle Bassan, the nurse. You'll find her number in the notebook beside the phone in the entrance hall. Tell her she won't have to come this evening, since a friend of ours has given Madame her injection."

"Yes, Mademoiselle."

The maid closed the door. Irène leaned her back against it with a slow, treacherous smile that gave Pascale a glimpse of a truth so horrible that she immediately tried to drive it out of her mind.

Andrea sat up on her pillows. She was still pale, but she seemed to have regained all her vitality. There was a disquieting gleam in her eyes.

Pascale stepped away from her.

"I . . . I don't understand. . . . You weren't unconscious? You didn't take an overdose of sleeping pills?"

"I have about fifteen minutes to live," Andrea said in her hoarse voice, "and you will have killed me. There's no use trying to call anyone. The phone in this room doesn't work, and the bell for the maid is beside Irène."

Pascale backed up to the fireplace and leaned against it. Her legs felt as if they were about to give way. Dark spots danced before her eyes and her ears were filled with the throbbing of her pulse.

Andrea's shrill laugh saved her from fainting. The objects around her gradually came back into focus. Her mind cleared and anger gave her new strength.

"You're the one who planned this!" she said to Irène. "If you don't call a doctor immediately, your sister will die in horrible agony!"

"Leave Irène alone," said Andrea. "She only carried out my orders, as usual. And since you have such a tender heart, you'll be glad to know that I'll die without pain. It's not your poison that will kill me, but another one that I took a few minutes before the injection. A poison whose presence can't be detected in the body. You're beginning to understand, aren't you? But there's something else you need to know. Death will be a deliverance for me. I have a cancer that would have killed me anyway, but after months of excruciating pain."

"That doesn't give you the right to kill yourself!" said Pascale.

Andrea laughed mockingly.

"I've always lived my life as I pleased, and now I'm ending it as I please. I've never cared whether I had a right to do anything or not. I've done what I wanted and left questions of right and wrong to sanctimonious fools like you."

"You're a monster," murmured Pascale.

"Why? Because my ideas are different from yours?"

"No. Because you've caused so much suffering. You—"

"I'm about to cause a lot more suffering," Andrea interrupted with hatred blazing in her eyes. "My death will be my revenge. First against Rémi, because he's not only treated Irène and me with contempt for the past eight years, but he's also refused to give us a share of his immense wealth.

"And then against you, Pascale. I know Rémi loves you; I knew it long before you did, you poor idiot. When I realized that my cancer would soon give the two of you a chance to be happy together, I decided to destroy your happiness completely. Rémi would have married you as soon as I was out of the way. But there's no chance of that now. All the evidence is against you, all of it! Even if Rémi is convinced you're innocent, and even if he's willing to wait till you get out of prison, however long that may be, it will still be impossible for him to marry the woman convicted of murdering his wife."

She broke into harsh laughter that ended as abruptly as it had begun.

Speechless with horror, Pascale looked at her as a sailor looks at a wave about to capsize his boat, without hatred, but with a feeling of total helplessness. She realized that she had to give up all hope of ever being happy again, that the despair now taking possession of her would never end.

"Ever since I left the hospital," gasped Andrea, "I've had a nurse come and give me an injection every day, so that—"

She suddenly fell back, with her eyes turned up. Irène rushed toward her. Pascale dashed to the door, opened it and ran down the stairs. In the entrance hall she feverishly picked up the telephone to call Dr. Bernier.

"YOUR STORY IS RIDICULOUS, Mademoiselle Nolay! Why don't you admit you typed that prescription on Monsieur Sévrier's typewriter? The *t* and the *d* are deformed enough to be clearly recognizable, and your fingerprints were found on the typewriter. You claim to have typed letters to six kennels, but no trace of any such letters has been found. Furthermore the date on the prescription is in your handwriting and the signature is forged. In view of all that, I can't understand why you go on denying the obvious facts."

Police Inspector Duval, the blond, amiable-looking giant who had come to the Sévriers' house in person after a telephone call from Dr. Bernier, was losing patience. He had been questioning Pascale Nolay for an hour and she still persisted in denying her crime in spite of the overwhelming evidence against her.

"According to Mademoiselle Deville, you were recently treated in Les Landes by the doctor whose name is on the prescription. Is that true?"

"Yes."

"And do you admit that you stole a prescription blank from him?"

"No."

Pascale added nothing. Although her face was haggard, she looked at Inspector Duval with calm self-assurance in her eyes.

The case was simple. Too simple, in fact. Duval, who was a personal friend of Rémi's, hesitated to set the implacable machine in motion, even though Pascale's story seemed totally implausible to him. She claimed that Irène had asked her to treat Andrea for an overdose of sleeping pills, but neither Irène nor the maid corroborated that claim. A few minutes before Pascale gave her the injection, Andrea had given the maid instructions for a party that was to take place the next evening. And on the writing desk in the very room where Duval was questioning Pascale, there was an unfinished letter, in Andrea's handwriting, inviting some friends to lunch the following week, which indicated that she had no thought of committing suicide.

When she had been confronted with all this evidence, Pascale had suddenly stopped trying to justify her conduct and begun answering Duval's questions only with a "yes" or a "no."

Rémi had been notified but he was in Algiers and wouldn't arrive in Versailles till the next day.

Maybe he'll throw some light on what happened, thought Inspector Duval. *But in the meantime, there's more than enough evidence against this woman to justify arresting her. Why should I hesitate? It's a classic case: an attractive, ambitious governess who kills her rich employer's wife in the hope of getting him to marry her later.*

That explanation didn't satisfy him. Something he saw in Pascale's eyes made it hard for him to believe she was capable of such a crime. But he had to disregard his personal feelings.

"You killed Madame Sévrier out of jealousy," he said harshly, "because she was the wife of the man you love."

Pascale winced as if he had slapped her. She closed her eyes and sat motionless for a long time, stiffened by unbearable pain.

She could easily have refuted Duval's argument by revealing Rémi's estrangement from Andrea, especially since Rémi himself would have supported her with his testimony as soon as he returned. But that would have meant betraying the secret he had carefully concealed for eight years. Not even Dr. Bernier, who was one of his friends, had known about Andrea's addiction and degradation.

"In your opinion, doctor," Inspector Duval had asked him, "can there be any doubt that the strychnine injection was the cause of Madame Sévrier's death?"

After a slight hesitation, Bernier had answered, "A strychnine solution can cause death under normal circumstances, although it acts as a beneficial stimulant in someone who's taken a heavy dose of a depressant drug."

If Pascale continued to say nothing, Rémi would be able to avoid a public scandal. It was the last proof of love she could give him.

But it was now becoming clear to her that her sacrifice had to be carried still further. Till now, she had denied killing Andrea. Rémi would know she wasn't lying, and he would try to save her by telling the truth about Andrea. With that new evidence to guide their investigation, the police would probably uncover the facts surrounding her death. Pascale would be exonerated, but at the cost of a terrible scandal for Rémi. He would be stigmatized, mocked, condemned and vilified, even by those who had respected him before. No, it was unthinkable. She had to protect him from all that.

She abandoned herself to the fervor of total self-sacrifice. She felt as if she were being enveloped and penetrated by a dazzling light.

She opened her eyes. Why did the people around her seem to be moving incredibly far away from her? And what was that police inspector saying to her through the dense fog that surrounded him?

"You killed her out of jealousy. Admit it."

"It's true," she said in a barely audible voice. "I killed Andrea Sévrier because I wanted to take her place."

She fainted and slid from her chair to the floor.

Chapter 17

When Pascale again became aware of the world around her, she was amazed at how weak she felt and didn't recognize the room in which she lay.

It was still a long time before her mind cleared completely. She then learned that she was in a Paris hospital and had been kept under heavy sedation for two days after her breakdown.

As soon as she seemed strong enough to talk about what had happened in Versailles, her mother told her the charges against her had been dismissed.

"But what about all the false evidence that Irène built up against me?" asked Pascale.

"Emmanuelle Nogares destroyed it," answered her mother. She paused hesitantly. "Are you sure you're ready to hear about it now? I'm afraid I may upset you too much by reminding you of things you'd rather forget."

Pascale shrugged indifferently.

"I'll be all right. Go ahead."

"Well, as soon as Emmanuelle heard about

Andrea's death she went to the police with a letter addressed to Irène that she'd found last summer at Estello. She'd read it, but hadn't told anyone about it because she was ashamed of being so inquisitive. In it, Andrea congratulated Irène for stealing a prescription blank from the doctor in Castarets when she went to his office to have her ankle examined. 'It may come in handy,' she wrote. She also referred to her incurable cancer and said, 'I don't have much longer to live, but at least I can make my death a vengeance.' That evidence, combined with Rémi's testimony, made the police question Irène again. She finally admitted everything. Only minor charges have been brought against her, since the fact is that Andrea did commit suicide."

Pascale's interest had been aroused by only one part of this story.

"What was Rémi's testimony?" she asked.

"He just told the truth about Andrea. That was enough! After all, she. . . ."

Pascale was no longer listening. Rémi had been forced to reveal his secret at last. Her attempt to spare him had been in vain. Her heart ached when she thought of what he must have endured.

She later learned that he had undertaken legal cases in several foreign countries and would be gone for many months.

Pascale went to Savoy for a vacation in the mountains and spent the whole winter there. At first she did nothing but rest and try to regain her interest in life, without much success. Then, when she had begun to worry about the financial strain she was putting on her mother, she went to work in a sanatorium, replacing a nurse who had been given a leave of absence till June.

THE TRAIN PULLED INTO the Versailles station.

Pascale, who had dozed off, woke up abruptly and gathered the pieces of her ticket strewn over her lap. The respite given her by sleep had been short. Her old sorrow gripped her once again.

As she was getting off the train, she hesitated. What was the sense of this pilgrimage? It would do nothing but exacerbate a pain that she had somehow learned to live with over the past eight months. If it hadn't been for the crowd pushing her away from the train, she might have turned back.

The day before, two days after her return to Paris, her mother had come across an ad in the newspaper: the Sévriers' house in Versailles was for sale. Those few words, read aloud, had released the flood of memories Pascale had been trying to keep dammed up. She had then announced her decision to go to Versailles the next day, to gather some personal belongings she had left there. It was a flimsy pretext that hadn't deceived anyone.

Lambert, who had come to the Nolays' apartment for lunch, had sadly turned his head away, but without protest. What good would it have done? He realized friendship didn't always lead to love. . . .

A moment after she stepped outside the station, Pascale stopped and stared in amazement. Serge, Rémi's chauffeur, bowed respectfully to her.

"Please follow me, Mademoiselle. The car is parked a little farther on."

She walked behind him like an automaton. The scene was so similar to the one that had taken place a year earlier that she felt as if she were dreaming. She tried to obtain an explanation from Serge but he deftly eluded her questions.

THE GRAVEL OF THE DRIVEWAY crunched beneath the wheels of the car. Reine, wearing a freshly ironed blue apron, was standing at the top of the front steps with a mischievous look on her face.

"Please come in, Mademoiselle."

She led Pascale to the study, where Rémi was waiting for her. He had been notified of her visit by a telephone call from her mother. He had been waiting for that call for a long time.

Although there were more strands of silver in his hair than before, his suntanned face seemed younger. He smiled tenderly and Pascale was warmed to the heart by the flame that danced in his ardent eyes. It was as if new blood had suddenly begun circulating in her veins.

She stood still for a few seconds, not daring to believe what she saw. Then two loving arms closed around her and she was submerged by a happiness unlike any other she had ever known.

They looked into each other's eyes in silence. No words could have expressed what they felt. Tears of joy welled up. He gently wiped them away, then his face leaned toward two lips that were learning to smile again. . . .

They were startled by the sound of frenzied barking from the entrance hall.

"That's Parky!" exclaimed Pascale. "If he's here, Etienne—"

"He must have just come back from his walk," Rémi interrupted with a smile. "I brought him here from the Nogares's farm, with Emmanuelle, when I found out you'd finally come back from Savoy. If you'd stayed much longer, he and I would have gone there to get you."

"I couldn't believe it was still possible for us to be happy," she confessed.

"I've always believed it, my darling. But we had to pay a heavy price for the right to be together. I knew our love would be strong enough to overcome anything but I felt we had to wait till the public's morbid curiosity had died down, and I wanted to give you time to recover from the terrible shock you suffered. As soon as I knew you were out of danger I left the country. But I asked your mother to write me about you without letting you know, while I was away.

"I'm not sure the morbid curiosity has completely died down yet, so we'll leave Versailles to avoid the gossip and slander. I've already bought a house in another suburb of Paris, a bright, cheerful house that will have only one secret in it: the secret of our happiness."

Two impatient fists hammered on the door.

"Come in," called Rémi.

Etienne burst into the room, followed by his dog, and skillfully tossed his cap onto the bust of Cicero. Then he stood still with his eyes open wide in amazement.

"Pascale!" he exclaimed, choking with emotion.

She leaned down. He threw his arms around her neck and kissed her.

"You're a little bit surprised, aren't you?" said Rémi, laughing.

Etienne could scarcely contain his joy but he managed to answer casually, "I'm not surprised at all. Parky told me she was here."

Rémi picked him up in his arms. With a kind of demanding tenderness, Etienne put out his hands and drew Rémi's and Pascale's faces together. He was silent for a moment, with a strangely somber expression. Then he murmured with deep anxiety, "Parky also told me you're never going to leave us again, Pascale. Is that true?"

"Parky never lies," answered Pascale.

"That dog always knows everything!" added Rémi.

They spoke with such wholehearted conviction that Etienne's fears flew away and he knew they would never return.

With happiness singing in his heart, he hugged them both as hard as he could.

See over for ordering information

Complete and mail this coupon today!

Order Form

Harlequin Reader Service
MPO Box 707
Niagara Falls, N.Y. 14302

In Canada:
649 Ontario St.
Stratford, Ont. N5A 6W2

Please send me the following Harlequin Mystiques. I am enclosing my check or money order for $1.50 for each novel ordered, plus 25¢ to cover postage and handling.

- ☐ **1. House of Secrets**
- ☐ **2. Vanishing Bride**
- ☐ **3. Proper Age for Love**
- ☐ **4. Island of Deceit**
- ☐ **5. High Wind in Brittany**
- ☐ **6. Love's Rebel**
- ☐ **7. The Master of Palomar**
- ☐ **8. Terror at Golden Sands**
- ☐ **9. The Law of Love**
- ☐ **10. In Search of Sybil**
- ☐ **11. Winter at Blackfont**
- ☐ **12. Bitter Honey**
- ☐ **13. Sisters at War**
- ☐ **14. The Whims of Fate**
- ☐ **15. By Love Forgotten**
- ☐ **16. The Sea Gull**

Number of novels checked _____ @ $1.50 each = $ _________

N.Y. and N.J. residents add appropriate sales tax $ _________

Postage and handling $ 25¢

TOTAL $ _________

NAME ____________________________
(Please print)

ADDRESS ____________________________

CITY ____________________________

STATE/PROV. ________________ ZIP/POSTAL CODE ________

Offer expires December 31, 1978

HMY 001